UFO Reports

Images of Elsewhere

Vol. IV

PETER LANG
Oxford - Berlin - Bruxelles - Chennai - Lausanne - New York

UFO Reports

Timothy Jenkins

PETER LANG
Oxford · Berlin · Bruxelles · Chennai · Lausanne · New York

Bibliographic information published by the Deutsche Nationalbibliothek.
The German National Library lists this publication in the German National Bibliography;
detailed bibliographic data is available on the Internet at http://dnb.d-nb.de.

A catalogue record for this book is available from the British Library.

Library of Congress Cataloging-in-Publication Data

Names: Jenkins, Timothy, 1952- author.
Title: UFO reports / Timothy Jenkins.
Description: Oxford; Bern; Berlin; Bruxelles; New York; Wien: Peter
   Lang, [2025] | Series: Images of elsewhere; vol. IV (4) | Includes
   bibliographical references and index.
Identifiers: LCCN 2024035330 (print) | LCCN 2024035331 (ebook) | ISBN
   9781803741673 (paperback) | ISBN 9781803741680 (ebook) | ISBN
   9781803741697 (epub)
Subjects: LCSH: Unidentified flying objects—Sightings and
   encounters—Research.
Classification: LCC TL789.J464 2025 (print) | LCC TL789.J464 2024 (ebook)
   | DDC 001.942—dc23/eng/20240806
LC record available at https://lccn.loc.gov/2024035330
LC ebook record available at https://lccn.loc.gov/2024035331

Cover image: Line drawing by the author.
Cover design by Peter Lang Group AG

ISBN 978-1-80374-167-3 (print)
ISBN 978-1-80374-168-0 (ePDF)
ISBN 978-1-80374-169-7 (ePub)
DOI 10.3726/b20807

© 2025 Peter Lang Group AG, Lausanne
Published by Peter Lang Ltd, Oxford, United Kingdom
info@peterlang.com - www.peterlang.com

Timothy Jenkins has asserted his right under the Copyright, Designs and Patents Act, 1988,
to be identified as Author of this Work.

All rights reserved.
All parts of this publication are protected by copyright.
Any utilisation outside the strict limits of the copyright law, without the permission of the
publisher, is forbidden and liable to prosecution.
This applies in particular to reproductions, translations, microfilming, and storage and processing
in electronic retrieval systems.

This publication has been peer reviewed.

Contents

Series Preface — vii

Introduction — 1

CHAPTER 1
Early controversies — 5

CHAPTER 2
George Adamski: A life — 43

CHAPTER 3
Machines and men — 103

Bibliography — 127

Index — 133

Series Preface

Reports of flying saucers – also known as UFOs – constitute a puzzle, for they are numerous, well attested, and hard to believe. There are tempting shortcuts to a 'solution' – that the sightings are real, or mistaken, or fictitious (made up) – but none of these prove satisfactory. Instead, we are brought to consider the history of sightings and the history, also, of how it became possible to regard such incidents in the terms that have become customary. Flying saucers in this fashion become a feature of the wider society, and allow an angle of approach to our modern, technological civilization: a small-scale problem that allows insight into the larger setting.

The six essays stand as independent studies. Each deals with an aspect of the life of flying saucers or UFOs: their appearance after the Second World War within the constellation of military and technological interests, their debt to early science fiction and its sources, the development of the search for signs of extra-terrestrial intelligence, the first adoptions of the 'interplanetary hypothesis' in civilian circles, the further expansion of reports, first, of sightings and, then, of abductions in the wider society, and, finally, a review of the range of forms which have appeared. Taken together, they form a thorough enquiry into reports of sightings of flying saucers.

The series as a whole makes three contributions to resolving the puzzle posed by such reports.

First, it relates three bodies of materials from the United States in the mid-twentieth century whose interactions must be taken into consideration when speaking about flying saucers. These are the science fiction milieu, the interplay of military and technical interests, and reports of sightings by members of the public; in short, stories, military work, and ordinary lives. The first contribution is to study their interactions, overlaps, borrowings and synergies.

The second is to derive the categories that are necessary to explain the convergence of these materials. Repeating patterns appear in science fiction literature, the history of Air Force intelligence in the Cold War period, the early days of NASA, the search for extra-terrestrial intelligence, and a wide variety of incidents and claims made by members of the public. To make sense of their common nature and to see how their interactions work, we also need to investigate some intellectual history. There is a longstanding tradition of popular thought putting new scientific discoveries and technological innovation to work for human moral purposes. This tradition was taken up by military and technical interests in the middle third of the twentieth century, using three clusters of ideas: the intimate connection between military technology and the world picture offered by modern media, the concept of 'communication' (and, post-War, of 'information') that became central in the period, and an understanding of 'memory' as an exact record of the past. These ideas were shared with a wider public: in the context of international tensions, hopes of communication and fears of its breakdown were given expression in the appearance of new forms of life, forms given content by the earlier longstanding history. This is the second contribution the essay makes to the topic: an investigation of the common patterns of thought necessary for stories, military work and ordinary lives to interact.

And, last, a mechanism is proposed by which these interactions occur. This is an analysis of the ways in which these 'images', which contain both real and imaginary elements, make their appearance compelling. I find well documented instances – in particular, the sessions in which memories of abductions are recovered – where the social mechanism is uncovered that allows the oscillation between the two elements, a mechanism that can be glimpsed at work in other sites but which cannot be tracked in such detail in the documents and other sources we have concerning advances in research, security decisions, the records of incidents and so forth. This is the third contribution.

I first came to the puzzle of flying saucer reports when working on spirit messages and similar forms of social life (such as parapsychology and psychical research) and realized that the search for extra-terrestrial intelligence was the latest expression of a long-held desire for communication with disembodied minds compatible with our own. It has taken a good deal of time and work to give substance to this insight. As will be clear from my references, there is an abundance of work of the highest quality

Series Preface ix

in this broad area, on which I draw to give shape to the argument. If I have contributed anything, it is by making a systematic enquiry and by putting together materials that are not always associated, and by continuing to ask questions rather than settling for accepted answers. In this fashion, I hope to have supported readers who find these topics interesting rather than those who wish to close them down, and I also hope to have contributed in some small degree to understanding the contemporary world.

Introduction

Flying saucers, slightly later called UFOs, first appeared in the early days of the Cold War, after the end of the Second World War in 1945. The combination of new weapons and new technologies of communication gave life to images that had first been imagined in pulp science fiction magazines in the earlier part of the twentieth century. And once hatched, they gained an independent existence, with their own rules as to potential and limits, influencing choices and decisions in the technical-military constellation that had given rise to them in the first place.[1]

What we are now concerned with is the life of these images once they got outside the environment in which they were generated. What happens to UFOs once they escape from being the concern of military intelligence and appear in civilian life? This exchange happened very early and, indeed, civilian responses played an important part in shaping military perceptions. The crucial point is that certain patterns of thought were transferred from the one sphere to the other. And, as these patterns were first produced in the military sphere, they were cast initially within a largely realistic – practical, pragmatic – view of the world, even though they later took different forms.

The transfer from the military to the civilian sphere can be traced through two case studies, which illustrate the principal forms of this exchange, conceived in terms, first, of the alternatives of truth or error and, second, of imaginative engagement. For the first pair proved unable on either side to produce conclusive results and, in the context of this impasse, other possibilities emerged.

The first chapter concerns two of the earliest figures who put the images created in the crucible of Air Force investigations to work in popular writings and who defined respectively the positive case for and the sceptical

---

1 See the first three essays of the series, *Flying Saucers – An Introduction, Religion and Science Fiction,* and *Martian Linguistics.*

case against the existence of flying saucers. Both figures – a former Marine officer, Donald Keyhoe, a distinguished Harvard astrophysicist, Donald Menzel – despite differences in background and education, shared certain characteristics and presuppositions; these included writing for pulp magazines in the 1930s and a view of the role of scientific language in allowing unambiguous communication on controversial topics. Together, they wrote out the initial terms on which flying saucers became part of public discussion and created the common framework of interpretation for public understanding of the phenomenon.

In the second chapter, I investigate the well-documented life of a 'contactee', George Adamski. I do so for two purposes. On the one hand, he provides the material for a detailed case study of the work of the imagination which is possible under the conditions described; his is an exemplary case. It also supports the argument for direct theosophical influence. On the other hand, his case provides insight into a range of other groups awaiting the arrival of flying saucers; the case study permits a sociological description of a more general kind, drawing out certain characteristics to be found in this kind of group and permitting a better understanding of these typical features. In particular, it allows a redescription of a form termed the 'paranoid style', showing positive aspects of this attitude of mind, including its appeal to others to join in a worldview constructed around a secret and to create new forms of social solidarity. It also makes the basis of this kind of social vocation appear, to wit, a naturalism that ignores social construction and promotes an account of language as possessing its own powers and activity, capable either of corrupting the world or reforming it. In short, we identify an energetic form of social life, capable of organizing and representing the world around in terms of secrecy and contagion; it is another form of moral accounting, a modern theodicy that is quite distinct from the picture proposed by Menzel and Keyhoe.

The two case studies present a range of what we may call commonplace ideas. These include, in no particular order, prestige, charisma, enquiry, suspicion, election and exclusion, duties and obligations (both to the wider society and to 'truth'), companionship, negotiation, building a party, lobbying, collecting (and manipulating) evidence, and handling financial interests; the list may be added to. The point is that these are all social ideas, concerned with relations between actors, who are making and appraising claims, continually placing themselves and their group with respect to other persons and institutions. Taken together, these ideas suppose a collective scene of action, a scene made up in large part of the things said and, behind them, common ways of thinking and judging.

Yet, these commonplace ideas are continually covered over by the actors who, as writers considering the action in which they have been involved, reduce the scene of action to the minds of thinking subjects. This particular description contains a specific claim, that any human scene can be understood by reference to the intentional acts of individual subjects; it is a claim often taken over by sociologists. But it is no more than a claim, for human individuality cannot be considered a basic given; it is, rather, produced by individual labour applied to collective material and supported by institutions. Beyond the case studies, then, our task is to give 'a clearer vocabulary for the description of human affairs' (Descombes 1992: 10).[2] The third chapter is concerned with reviewing these empirical materials to discern the more abstract patterns that emerge from them, seeking sociological insight into these common ways of thinking and judging.

When we move to civilian reports, we find that seeing new objects is linked to the appearance of new forms of apprehension, and that these mobile forms emerge within a realist mode of description but alter, or even undermine, its realistic properties. Out of the first chapter, then, I identify two forms of social logic: a claim of objective truth ('the flying saucers are real') and denial of this claim ('this is a case of mistaken identity'). But both claim and denial serve as moves within a deeper game. They are both ways of grasping appearances, promoting certain understandings and repressing other elements.

We can call them styles of representation, which may be labelled 'organic' and 'mechanical' respectively, or narrative and structure. In short, claims for the reality of UFO reports are principally narrative forms, which are usually denied in terms of a structural – or scientific – perspective, an

---

2   The argument presented in these two paragraphs draws on Descombes (1992). It may be added, the situation is made formally more complex in the case of these three figures because of the presence of non-human intentional actors.

explaining away ('you think you have seen x, but in fact the explanation is y'). Both forms of representation, however, leave out something vital; neither is sufficient to understand the simultaneous emergence of new objects and the shift in understanding that accompanies their appearance. Narrative hints at this fluidity, while structure refuses it. In support of this view, the initial claim is always put in terms of proclaiming a 'new' truth, and the objections, while posed in a realistic idiom, are principled denials of the imaginative energy being expressed.

We therefore need to invoke a third kind of social logic, the energetic nature of sightings 'prior' to their being caught up in representations of either kind. Sightings in this regard are understood as the point of encounter between populations and the production of affects in both parties. In this fashion, a different account of patterns of disturbance can be identified and explored. In sum, in the last chapter I describe three kinds of social logic, forms which are still held within the compass of realistic description but testing its limits.

In this essay, then, we follow the early transfer of a range of possible forms of understanding from the military sphere to the civilian, conceived, first, in terms of the opposition of truth to error and, second, in the imaginative work that both underlies those alternatives and can outbid both. And we seek to identify the different kinds of social logic that allow this range of forms.

CHAPTER 1

Early controversies

The earliest sightings of flying saucers or UFOs were in military circles, where they gave rise to well-defined images with particular properties. Our concern, however, is to consider reports of sightings made by members of the public, people outside the military-technical establishment, and the reception of these reports, which were always controversial. In this chapter, I look at two early figures whose work and experience were only possible because of the constructions put together by Air Force intelligence between 1947 and 1953 (although we also go a bit beyond that period); each played a role in the interactions of the security establishment with the public arena and the shift of the flying saucer from one sphere to the other. The two form a pair: the first, Donald Keyhoe, was the original public advocate of the 'interplanetary hypothesis', while the second, Donald Menzel, an astrophysicist, put forward a contrary position, proposing all the observed phenomena were capable of natural explanation. Each was well aware of the other; together, they laid down the framework of rival interpretations which were then to hand to cover over the usually small-scale disturbances provoked by civilian sightings. Despite their conflicting views, the pair show not only contrasts but also similarities of approach. Their debates open the way for consideration of other figures, in the next chapter, a contactee, George Adamski, and (in other materials, not considered here) testimony from members of the public who made reports of sightings through journalists. These witnesses, however, drew increasingly different materials into the mix.

I. Truth claims

Donald Keyhoe (1897–1988) was one of the first journalists to research the flying saucer phenomenon, publishing an article in *True* magazine at the end of 1949 titled 'The Flying Saucers Are Real' (Keyhoe 1950a). This article is credited with establishing the interplanetary hypothesis in the public mind. He turned the article into a book using the same title the following year (Keyhoe 1950b), which is reputed to have sold over half a million copies (see Jacobs 1975: 57; Peebles 1994: 39; Clark 1998: 326; Swords and Powell 2012: 75).

Keyhoe continued to play a significant role in ufology for the next twenty years, publishing four more books (Keyhoe 1953, 1955, 1960, 1973) and helping found and then leading what was claimed to be the largest and most influential civilian UFO research group in the US in the decade from the late fifties. This was the National Investigations Committee on Aerial Phenomena (NICAP), founded in 1956, which gathered a range of prominent scientists, military and professional people, published a newsletter, and lobbied Congress for hearings and investigations into the existence of UFOs and the Air Force's handling of the question. Keyhoe was a major actor in the field of UFO investigations from 1949 to 1969.

He had a background in early military aviation; he was trained in the Naval Academy in Annapolis, being commissioned lieutenant in the Marine Corps in 1919. He retired from the Marines in 1923, having been injured in a plane crash, although he returned to active duty in the Second War, serving in the Naval Aviation Training Division and retiring with the rank of major (Clark 1998: 325f.). This is how he presented himself in the post-War writings, as 'Major Donald E. Keyhoe, U.S. Marine Corps (ret.)' (from the front cover of Keyhoe 1953). In the 1920s and 1930s, he went through a series of jobs, emerging as a writer of pulp stories and journalism. He was then well placed regarding the skills and knowledge peculiar to each trade, pulp writing, military life in its technological aspects, and journalistic investigation, which played their parts in the second part of his career. We shall look briefly in turn at the pulp fiction, the first writings on flying saucers, and the work of NICAP. We shall draw in discussion of Menzel's work after consideration of Keyhoe's first book, for Menzel's work in some regards constitutes a reply to Keyhoe's claims, and we shall consider some of their shared presuppositions.

'Philip Strange'

Pulp writing may be said to have contributed an enduring attitude of mind. Keyhoe wrote for pulp magazines for more than ten years from 1925, publishing several dozen stories (including early pieces in *Weird Tales*). I have read a single volume of his stories, stories originally published in *Flying Aces* magazine in 1931 and 1932 and recently republished (Keyhoe 2011), which recount the fictional adventures of a First World War pilot on the Western Front. They feature Philip Strange, who worked for G-2, an army air intelligence unit. Strange had an exotic past, including an unhappy childhood when, an orphan, his gifts were exploited as a stage mentalist, and he later travelled in the East, where he developed his mental and martial abilities. When he emerged in the intelligence business, he was notable not only for his practical capabilities at fighting and flying, nor simply his cosmopolitan skill at disguising himself, but also for his mental 'sensitivity' – his power of sensing the intentions and reading the minds of others which reached the level of telepathy, his ability to focus both mind and body in a crisis, learnt from yogic practice, and his talent both to mesmerize others and to resist hypnotism. He made a formidable opponent.

Keyhoe's early writing cannot be completely detached from his later, post-Second War work on flying saucers because he carried over some themes or, at least, some parallels emerge. In the first place, each story begins with a mystery to be solved, usually a form of attack that implies the enemy has unusual, even supernatural, powers: pilots are found dead without a mark on them; entire squadrons become demoralized, afflicted by cowardice, fights between comrades, and suicides; there is even the appearance of a ghostly pterodactyl which destroys aircraft in the air and on the ground. Yet second, behind this supernatural guise, one may discern human technical activity at work. Beyond the 'normal' deceptions practised between enemies, concerning spies and traitors, misinformation and sabotage, the enemy uses technical means to produce these supernatural illusions, either to disguise the secret weapons he is deploying or directly to affect morale. Third, therefore, by good intelligence work, the agent – Strange – can put together the evidence and decipher the enemy's activity, unmasking both the deception and the innovation and putting an end to its effectiveness. But this can only be done retrospectively: apparently supernatural riddles must be read correctly after the event, to allow appropriate practical countermeasures to be taken; this is the structure of each narrative. There is no pre-emptive intelligence possible, for the uncanny nature of the phenomenon forbids it.

There is then in each story an enemy conspiracy which includes its own techniques of disguising itself, for both the secret weapon and the concealment are technological inventions; often, indeed, the manipulation of appearances is the weapon being employed. There is a secret to be deciphered behind appearances. Some deceptions are simply camouflage, as in chemical smoke protecting the enemy mountain valley hideaway, or a zeppelin painted matt black to be invisible at night; others involve sabotage by agents or traitors, so that pilots are killed by poison smeared on their controls, or demoralized patients killed by tampered-with injections. In another case, however, mass demoralization is caused by the insinuation of secret codes behind the Morse patterns the pilots are learning during sleep using headphones, so that instructions for the next day are conveyed through the power of hypnotism and suggestion, instructions which furthermore conceal themselves by ordering the subjects to forget the source of their programmed behaviour. And the pterodactyl's destructive effects arise from the use of electromagnetic coils to break up planes by their repulsive effects, or to draw them near, into the grasp of the dummy's mechanical claws, worked from the invisible zeppelin from which the ghostly machine is suspended, allowing its manoeuvres and silent flight.

The secrets may be crude, but they are concerned with the technical manipulation of both mental and material powers, with advanced technologies that simultaneously create effects in the world and control the perception of these effects. They balance mental and military elements, affecting bodies and minds equally, attacking morale as much as ground positions. Action at a distance, whether 'mind-stealing' or electromagnetic, is as significant as engagement body-to-body. We may suspect that, to see through the deceptions of this semiotechnical order, the gifted individual needs his highly trained mental and physical abilities, products of a curious past, to stand a chance with the human conspiracies against which he is pitted.

All the narratives are told in clipped prose, made up of short sentences containing plenty of Forces' jargon and slang, phrases conveying information in an authoritative form and with heightened emotion, recounting frequent reversals of fortune and suspense but leading, nevertheless, to Strange's invariable victory over the odds.

It is not over-imaginative to see the same narrative pattern at work in Keyhoe's unveiling of the Air Force's dilemmas, confronted with the appearance of flying saucers and their combination of physical and mental properties.

The Flying Saucers Are Real

It is striking that the form of the plot – penetrating technologically-created appearances to discern organized conspiracies – persists in Keyhoe's journalistic work when he approached the question of flying saucers. He had developed a career as a freelance writer in the aviation field (Jacobs 1975: 56), replacing that of pulp author, writing on topics such as 'Axis espionage and Communist activities' and going so far as detecting secret German plans of which he claimed the FBI had cognisance (Peebles 1994: 37). He used the same approach in the *True* article (Keyhoe 1950a), developed in more detail in the book, where the overall narrative structure is organized around his journalistic investigation for the article, and begins from the puzzle presented by inconsistencies in the official accounts. We might also remark continuity in the style, as in this brief example: 'The mysterious object streaked vertically skyward, hovered for a while miles above the earth, and then disappeared' (Keyhoe 1950b: 13).[1]

His principal theses are these: that flying saucers are spaceships from another planet (or planets); that they have been observing the earth for at least two hundred years, though their observations have increased since the explosion of atomic weapons; and that there is no indication that they intend to move from observation to contact (see the summary in Keyhoe 1950b: 174). Much of the book is devoted to a narrative of how he came to this conclusion: how he became aware of the problem, how pieces of the evidence fell into place, and how his initial scepticism became converted into this conviction.

In this narrative, he covers much the same material as Ruppelt's book (Ruppelt 1956), Edward Ruppelt being the officer leading Air Force intelligence gathering on flying saucers. Keyhoe cites all the early classic cases, returning repeatedly to the Mantell incident which he sees as providing a key to the whole story of Air Force involvement and strategy with respect to flying saucers (Keyhoe 1950b: 158). He also establishes the character of each of the main witnesses and actors. He offers an account of divisions within the Air Force as to what policy to adopt, speculatively because he lacked Ruppelt's access to the official documents. He weaves in accounts of earlier sightings from the nineteenth century, drawing in part on Fort's writings, and those prior to Arnold in the twentieth: foo fighters and Swedish rockets (I believe he is the first to incorporate these materials). He delineates the series of discarded candidates – Soviet or German weapons or United States prototypes – leading to the interplanetary hypothesis as the other possibilities are counted out (a method of residues leading to a known unknown), and he touches on the role of radar in convincing sceptics of the reality of flying saucers and providing evidence of intelligent manoeuvres on the part of the saucers.

One feature is that the detail of the interplanetary hypothesis is worked out by reasoning back from developing human technology and by anticipating how we might expect to respond to space travel and the possibility of encountering other civilizations. He works on analogies

---

[1] Keyhoe (1950b) read online; the pagination taken from Project Gutenberg Ebook.

drawn from contemporary technological development, and has a discussion of possible flying saucer design features; this short passage gives the tenor of the ideas:

> They may be powered with atomic energy or by the energy that produces cosmic rays – which is many times more powerful – or by some other fuel or natural force that our research hasn't yet discovered. But the circular aerofoil is quite feasible.
>
> It wouldn't have the stability of the conventional aeroplane, but it would have enormous manoeuvrability – it could rise vertically, hover, descend vertically, and fly at extremely high speed, with the proper power. (Keyhoe 1950b: 88)

It is taken for granted that the visitors will be representatives of a 'higher race' (Keyhoe 1950b: 64), hundreds or even thousands of years ahead of us (Keyhoe 1950b: 109), although he also notes that if, as scientists discuss, there may be a range of life on other planets, some races will be less advanced than Earth (Keyhoe 1950b: 119). And he reasons that, with respect to these higher life forms, their behaviour probably resembles ours: they will observe without contact, test conditions, and follow our progress from a distance. It is effectively a parallel intelligence operation. For their interest lies in Earth's technological development over the last two hundred years and has been heightened by the recent acceleration of activity – the Second World War, atomic explosions, and high-altitude experiments in rocket flight (Keyhoe 1950b: 132). He correlates the history of their past visits and present focus on the United States with this interpretation, including their concentration on sites of strategic and military interest.

In line with this narrative, Keyhoe proposes that three kinds of craft have been observed: 'Type I, a small nonpilot-carrying disk-shaped aircraft equipped with some form of television or impulse transmitter; Type II, a very large, metallic, disk-shaped aircraft operating on the helicopter principle; Type III, a dirigible-shaped, wingless aircraft that, in the Earth's atmosphere, operates in accordance with the Prandtl theory of lift' (Keyhoe 1950b: 142). There are distant large motherships and the smaller craft they release for closer surveys, manned and unmanned, through which they observe and test air defences but do not engage in contact. If, ultimately, they make contact, what will they be like? Keyhoe speculates they will be like us: intelligent, courageous, and curious; not belligerent, but painstaking and methodical (Keyhoe 1950b: 137).

At the same time, he proposes an equally important secondary thesis, that the Air Force have already followed this path of deciphering the evidence and have gained a dawning conviction as to the provenance of the machines, and that they have developed, for reasons of public order, a double strategy of, on the one hand, denying the existence of flying saucers, to prevent panic, and, on the other, of preparing the public for this new revelation by a series of leaks. He notes the role of the Orson Welles' 1938 broadcast as exemplifying the threat of panic. This inferred pair of potentially contradictory aims allows the interpretation of any Air Force statement within the proposed frame. Indeed, the primary materials Keyhoe employs to establish his first thesis are the various Air Force statements (press releases) concerning the early cases, and his evidence for the second in the main comprises readings of the contradictions between the two parts of their supposed strategy as the Air Force is held to advance or retreat in its aims according to circumstance. In this fashion, he traces the development of Project Grudge and its predecessor, identifying the early history of investigation and secrecy from 1947, with the addition of the second aim of alerting the public in the spring of 1949, and mapping the oscillations around these aims in the explanations offered for the Mantell, Chiles-Whitted and Gorman cases (1950b: 173).

The second concern – the detection of a (benign) government and Air Force cover-up together with a strategy of public education – is the optic through which the first concern is presented. There is no remainder – no materials independent of the Air Force reports – and Keyhoe makes full play of his Service contacts with Pentagon officials. Their denials of any cover-up convince him only of the importance and coordination of the strategy, which must then be organized at the highest levels. The frame of interpretation allows every detail to be incorporated in a narrative, and each seeming contradiction is presented either as a shift towards greater openness or as a return to the priority of secrecy. Keyhoe concludes: 'I believe that the Air Force is still investigating the saucer sightings, either through the Air Material Command or some other headquarters. It is possible that some Air Force officials still fear a panic when the truth is officially revealed. In that case, we may continue for a long time to see routine denials alternating with new suggestions of interplanetary travel' (1950b: 174).

The focus throughout is then as much on 'Project Saucer' – the name used in contemporary press releases for the Air Force group responsible – as it is on their investigations, and with their inferred tasks of repressing the truth and preparing the public, explaining away the reports and yet putting out contradictory statements: 'Project "Saucer" was trying hard to explain away the sightings and hide the real answer' (Keyhoe 1950b: 87). Keyhoe discredits various of the explanations offered, pointing out their inconsistencies, and also identifies possible coincidences in the timing of official announcements – he juxtaposes the announcement of a commitment to space research with one denying the existence of flying saucers – as implying high level coordination.

Keyhoe can present himself and his journalistic efforts as both being in the know and aiding the Air Force strategy; the reception of the *True* article, for instance, can offer a lesson that the American people are curious but not panicked on the topic of flying saucers. However, Keyhoe also links the discovery of saucers with the potential development of human space flight and rocketry and suggests that secrecy concerning the one may be tied to secrecy about the other. Despite these considerations, he believes that 'Americans cannot escape eventual contact with dwellers on other planets. Even though space visitors never attempt to contact us, sooner or later earthlings will be travelling to distant planets – planets the scientists have said are almost surely inhabited'. His final words are these: 'The American people have proved their ability to take incredible things. We have survived the stunning impact of the Atomic Age. We should be able to take the Interplanetary Age, when it comes, without hysteria' (Keyhoe 1950b: 175).

In short, Keyhoe's article and book take every feature of the developing narrative of the Air Force's involvement with flying saucers and give it definitive form, notably by taking the interplanetary hypothesis for granted and focussing attention on the evasions believed to have been effected by human official forces. We might also note that he realizes the theosophical agenda without remainder, populating the story with state, military, and other actors, some drawn from other planets.[2]

2   See the second essay, *Religion and Science Fiction*.

II. Explanations of error

Donald Menzel (1901–1976) was professor of Astrophysics at Harvard[3] when he wrote *Flying Saucers*, published by Harvard University Press in 1953. His thesis is that all reports of flying saucers can be explained, either as reflections from objects in the air, such as newspapers, balloons or distant aeroplanes, or as ground lights reflected in a thin haze or layer of cloud, or as reflections and refractions produced by drops of water, ice crystals or layers of air. In short, 'all reports of saucers … result from unusual and unfamiliar conditions in the atmosphere' (Menzel 1953: 272). His contribution lies in identifying the products of miscellaneous meteorological optics, 'mirages, reflections in mist, refractions and reflections by ice crystals' (Menzel 1953: vii), a category that the Air Force group given the task of investigating flying saucer reports had missed entirely (Menzel 1953: 10). His principal conclusions are negative: we are not dealing with military devices, either American or Russian, and 'above all, there is not the slightest evidence to support the popular fantasy that saucers are interplanetary space ships, manned by beings from beyond the earth' (Menzel 1953: vii–viii).

Menzel's 'Flying Saucers'

Menzel is well worth listening to, for his expertise lay in astronomy and meteorology and, in addition, he had been involved in the development of naval radar during the Second War, dealing with practical technical problems in the Pacific (Menzel 1953: 268) and later serving as Chairman of the Wave Propagation Committee of the Joint Chiefs of Staff (Menzel 1953: 218). A critic suggested that the book could be read as a popular introduction to meteorology disguised as a work on flying saucers. Menzel however also shows a good acquaintance with the classical sightings, as

---

3 For a biography, see 'Donald Howard Menzel' at encyclopedia.com, accessed 17 August 2020.

well as with the history of the topic including earlier reports of wonders, and a certain literary flair. Moreover, he does not confine himself to accounting for sightings, but also offers criticisms of the Air Force handling of reports, and he explains the popularity of the interplanetary hypothesis as the other side of his scientific method. The book joins together several strands of argument.

It is worth remarking his ability as a popular science writer, for Menzel too served an apprenticeship in pulp magazines. He was a regular columnist in Hugo Gernsback's range of popular journals which combined articles on recent scientific and technological advances with stories, the earliest forms of science fiction. He contributed 'speculative articles of a radical nature' (Ashley and Lowndes 2004: 145), with titles such as 'Can we visit the planets?' (1924, writing as Don Home), 'Can we signal Mars?' (1925, as Charles T. Dahama), 'The End of the World' (1924), 'The Mystery of Atomic Energy' (1925), and a series on 'Space, Time & Relativity' in 1929. He served as an advisor to Gernsback's *Amazing Stories* (founded in 1926) in the late 1920s (Ashley and Lowndes 2004: 96), and reviewed stories submitted to the range of magazines (Ashley and Lowndes 2004: 143). His only recorded pieces of science fiction (from Ashley's research), however, were 'The Machine from Outside' (under the name Don Howard) in *Weird Tales* in 1924, and a later piece, 'The Other Side of Zero', in *Science-Fiction Plus* in 1953 (Ashley and Lowndes 2004: 145).

Returning to his 1953 book, he presents his case in the first five chapters by developing three main theses: that we are dealing in natural phenomena, and so there have always been instances of this kind of thing; that there is a history of misidentification of these instances, myths and superstitions which persist today; and that, in the present age, scientific explanations can be provided for the phenomena, so the myths may be discarded. In the remaining chapters, he develops each thesis in more detail. I will outline his initial discussion, before reviewing the later materials more briefly.

He begins by citing Kenneth Arnold's sighting as a typical case, offering two possible meteorological explanations based on the mountainous terrain, either blasts of snow, billowing from the ridges in waves and catching the sunlight, or, in a similar fashion, layers of dust reflecting the sun and twisted by the violent air circulation. 'I feel certain that turbulence over the ridge ... was in the main responsible for Arnold's saucers. But whether the apparent metal glint came from billows of snow or billows of haze we do not have enough evidence ... to decide' (Menzel 1953: 10).

Menzel's strategy is then to disaggregate 'saucer' reports and to offer a heterogeneous range of explanations, although the meteorological ones occupy him mainly, in large part because insufficiencies in the Air Force classification which, while it deals in mistaken identifications of man-made objects, the misrecognition of astronomical phenomena, and 'hallucinations in general', has no place for the effects of mist, ice crystals or mirages. He offers several criticisms, indeed, of Air Force handling of their enquiries – the restriction of information which might have led to scientific explanations if freely available (Menzel 1953: 2), their mishandling of early enquiries (Menzel 1953: 18–19) which led to suspicions of a cover-up in the Mantell (Menzel 1953: 21–22) and Maury Island (Menzel 1953: 42) incidents, and the ambiguous wording of some press releases which appear to authorize the interplanetary hypothesis (Menzel 1953: 47). These complaints may be conceding necessary ground to Keyhoe (1950b).

In the early chapters, he runs over the classic sightings by pilots ('saucers from the air') and types of ground sightings ('saucers from the ground'), introducing the kind of explanations he will examine in more detail later in the book. He starts from mirages arising from the optical properties of air temperature 'inversions' (a layer of hotter air beneath a colder) and uses the behaviour of mirages with respect to an observer to suggest solutions to foo fighters (Menzel 1953: 18), the Chiles-Whitted case (Menzel 1953: 14) and the Gorman dogfight (Menzel 1953: 16–18). He also discusses the Mantell case (Menzel 1953: 20–21) in terms of the pilot's pursuit of a 'mock sun' or 'sundog', a patch of reflected sunlight caused by ice crystals in cirrus cloud which, like the mirages, may respond to movements of the observer and so appears to show intentional behaviour. In terms of ground sightings, he begins with objects seen in daylight, moving in winds at high levels, such as skyhook balloons carrying meteorological instruments (Menzel 1953: 26). But there are also instances of mirages created by cloud or smoke, as well as air temperature inversions, with reflections of objects such as a plane, a balloon, or of the rising or setting sun being distorted, doubled and so forth (Menzel 1953: 26–33). At night, saucers appear as lights in the sky, singly or in groups, sometimes in formation (as in the Lubbock lights); these echelons may be distant lights from beyond the horizon reflected in 'a rippling layer of haze, probably just over the heads of the observers' (Menzel 1953: 36). Such a series of lights may also give the impression of windows along a fuselage, while green balls of fire flashing by are probably meteorites (Menzel 1953: 38). Menzel also notes that sightings in the West and Southwest (where there are several sensitive sites) are assisted by 'the extreme clarity of the atmosphere in these regions' as compared with the East and the cities (Menzel 1953: 26).

Having given us a tour of the kind of phenomena that will concern us, and after a brief review of hoaxes (setting up a later important discussion of why deceptions can persist), Menzel offers the reader an outline of his method, in a chapter entitled 'The scientific detective'. Since there are many honest reports (he gives a chart of unexplained sightings between 1947 and 1952 – Menzel 1953: 58), the problem falls into two questions: What has been seen? And what is the frame of interpretation being used?

To take the second question first, why do people pose the matter in terms of interplanetary spacecraft? Menzel proposes an explanation in several parts. First, Americans like being scared – 'frightened in a shivery sort of way' – and will resent losing this illusion if told saucers are natural phenomena. He calls this liking 'a desire to make science fiction come true' (Menzel 1953: 49). But second, he suggests, there is also a widespread belief that 'regard[s] the flying saucers as real, manned space craft' (Menzel 1953: 49–50), a movement with its own leaders, supported by articles in various reputable magazines which give 'so-called explanations, full of high-sounding phrases … [and] meaningless jargon – pseudoscientific double talk' (Menzel 1953: 50). He must have Keyhoe in mind, although other publications were appearing. This belief is supported by a third element, a distrust on the part of these 'cultists' of the motives and truthfulness of scientists, the Air Force, the Atomic Energy Commission, and government circles.

Menzel calls this distrust 'religious' in nature, a tactic to defend flying saucers as 'a religious symbol, perhaps a proof of the existence of a power beyond the skies', and sees it at work in the notion that scientists and others are concealing what they know, either to gain the secrets of saucer propulsion or because they have captured some 'little men who survived a saucer crash in New Mexico ... [whom] we want to force ... to give us the scientific information that their super brains have evolved'. Under these circumstances, he remarks, 'the mere fact of denial lends credence to the ideas' (Menzel 1953: 50).

Here we have some familiar elements, science fiction inputs leading to an elusive but widespread unorthodox belief, fed by the press, and defended by a world view that distrusts authority. In various places, Menzel links this attitude of mind to primitive beliefs and superstition; indeed, he begins the essay in this fashion: '*Throughout the ages, apparitions of one kind or another have plagued* the human race. Primitive people the world over have generally believed in the existence of demons, ghosts, elves, goblins, dragons, sea serpents – to mention just a few of the more common fantasies' (Menzel 1953: 1).

He therefore assimilates flying saucer 'beliefs' to a permanent state of the primitive mind in the style of a comparative religion approach – a fear of thunder attributed to 'some pagan god' (Menzel 1953: 4), the 'mumbo jumbo' of alchemy (Menzel 1953: 25), 'our prehistoric ancestors personalizing all the forces of nature' (Menzel 1953: 51), the 1897 lights causing 'a religious sensation, many of the superstitious believing the end of the world was at hand' (Menzel 1953: 65), 'superstitious and often illiterate natives mistaking light reflections for fire spirits' (Menzel 1953: 103), 'fortune tellers, oracles, and soothsayers flourished, preying upon the superstitious ignorance of their fellow men' (Menzel 1953: 106), and so forth. While he places this primitive cast of mind, capable of blaming every 'seemingly inexplicable fact ... on an outside force over which we have no control' (Menzel 1953: 51), firmly in the province of the psychologist (Menzel 1953: 53), there is nevertheless a more radical remedy: it can be corrected by an appeal to the scientific method. 'We who live in the age of science know we should observe the world through rational, scientific eyes. Science has taught us not to fear the shooting star ... not to hold an eclipse or a comet responsible for disaster' (Menzel 1953: 135).

Here then Menzel returns to the first question: what has in fact been seen? And he introduces a composite figure as a protagonist, the 'scientific detective', made up of the detective Sherlock Holmes combined with the scientist Henri Poincaré: we must eliminate the impossible, and choose the simplest hypothesis to explain the observational data. Menzel acknowledges that the flying saucer enthusiast believes he is making the same moves but, he points out, while the scientist appeals to the known, the enthusiast makes appeal to some yet unknown explanatory cause, 'conclud[ing] that some superhuman intelligence must be responsible' (Menzel 1953: 51).

We might remark on the emblematic use of Sherlock Holmes as a model for the scientific approach,[4] for it is a sign that the writer has not heard the case the enthusiast is making. Holmes is the arch-positivist: human behaviour is rule-governed, just as are the scientific methods Holmes employs in his detection. What is more, you can deduce both the past actions of a person and predict their future behaviour by reconstructing their rational processes of thought, which work along functionalist lines. This line of thought dovetails with the comparative approach to traditional belief which, although made up of examples of irrational (non-utilitarian) thought can, nevertheless, can be anticipated by the scientist. Rationalism and its comparative supplement together form a complete mind-set.

Yet this form of scientific optimism is precisely what the flying saucer enthusiast is challenging. On the one hand, there is a philosophical challenge - although this is not much heard - for without a 'grammar' or set of patterns, you cannot explain whether a chain of thoughts is logical or illogical. And while the association of ideas - the mechanism allowing a comparative approach - makes appeal to a utilitarian or functionalist account, this is little more than a gesture; it cannot explain rational thought (cf. Descombes 2001).

On the other hand, it was felt that twentieth-century realities no longer supported the kind of world demanded by the deductive method, exemplified by Holmes' claim that 'when you have eliminated the impossible, whatever remains, however improbable, must be the truth' (*The Sign of Four* - cited by Menzel 1953: 51). The problem could be expressed in a number of versions: that after the First World War, civilization no longer upheld an order which would allow deduction of this kind to operate and

---

4 Peebles (1994) - a sceptical account - has a citation from Holmes stories as an epigraph for each chapter.

that the world showed more 'mental' kinds of properties; that the advances of the sciences in the twentieth century show a parallel variation of this view with the involvement of the observer with the phenomena observed; and that, particularly after the Second War, as technology controls all aspects of life including the means of apprehending reality, appearances may well be shaped to conceal their underlying motive causes. By appealing to Holmes, Menzel seeks to demythologize all versions of this modernist account of the world: his position comes down to an appeal to trust in the positivist worldview of 'science', and to reject any desire to embody a more contemporary understanding as 'primitive'.

In short, Menzel limits the effectiveness of his naturalistic explanations (which are, by and large, telling) by appealing to a positivist frame to explain why these explanations are not readily heard and accepted.

As he concludes this core chapter, he returns to the arguments advanced in support of the interplanetary hypothesis: the metallic appearance of many sightings, their speed and power of acceleration, the inference of non-human bodies capable of withstanding these forces, and the seemingly intelligent piloting of the craft, anticipating and parrying human responses. And he proposes, first, that we suppose the phenomena are not material – and therefore not manned – and second, that they may depend on the reflection of natural phenomena which respond to the human viewpoint, in effect, mimicking human actions (see Menzel 1953: 54–56). These phenomena may be understood on the model of the rainbow: 'the saucers, then, are only patterns of light, no more substantial than the squares of sunlight falling on the floor of my study. They are as real as the shadow that follows me on a sunny day and no more solid. Small wonder that all attempts to capture a saucer have led to naught!' (Menzel 1953: 56). It all comes down to learning not to trust one's perceptions; as he says elsewhere, 'a significant fallacy lies in the maxim "seeing is believing"' (Menzel 1953: 170). He closes the chapter with an extract from Poe's story 'The Sphinx', to make the point that perspective and distance relative to background can radically alter the narrative offered of perceptions.

The three theses revisited

In the following chapters, he presents a series of case studies reinforcing his three main claims, first, that these are natural phenomena, and therefore can be traced in historical materials; second, that they have a history of being wrongly interpreted, sometimes to ill effect, and that this history of misinterpretation continues to the present; and third, that contemporary scientific understandings can lay these ghosts.

With regard to the first claim, he runs through some eclectic materials for evidence of earlier sightings, drawing in part on Fort ('the best reference to ancient saucers' – Menzel 1953: 58), discussing the 1897 airship sightings (which Keyhoe had drawn into the debate) and a Greenwich Observatory report of a torpedo-shaped disk in 1882, as well as a report from *Nature* of 1893 of lights following a ship in the North China seas. In each case, he has meteorological solutions to offer: in the first, the planet Venus and the star Alpha Orionis are possible candidates, as well as a lenticular cloud; in the second, an unusual auroral display, and in the third, a mirage of distant lights reflected in a thin layer of frost crystals. He also scatters in discussion of a Fortean miscellany of other phenomena, from green fireballs to luminous bats.

He then pursues evidence of such sightings further back, dealing with material from the seventeenth and eighteenth centuries (which in turn refer to earlier reports), which allow him to draw in the challenge that Newton's account of natural phenomena offered to a view that linked signs in the sky to human affairs. He detects a shift in a treatise by a Jesuit, Franz Reinzer, published in 1709, who combined detailed, illustrated descriptions – details which permit Menzel to offer re-descriptions in meteorological terms – with, nevertheless, interpretations which transferred natural – meteorological – qualities to men and moral qualities to meteors (see Menzel 1953: 113). The main lesson of such erudite research is that, although the records are often hard to interpret, these unusual heavenly phenomena have always been observed, a thesis which is vital to the naturalistic approach adopted by the scientific detective.

He concludes this historical section with a reading of Ezekiel's vision (Ezekiel 1 and 10), which he explains by reference to sundogs or mock suns and their associated halos, a phenomenon produced by reflections from ice crystals in the atmosphere. He goes on to associate this meteorological interpretation with the seraphim in Isaiah 6, with Daniel's vision of four great beasts (Daniel 7; in this case, perhaps, mock moons), and with much of the imagery of Revelation. This chapter is a tour de force.

This historical investigation of records of earlier phenomena has sufficiently introduced the second thesis, that earlier accounts are 'obscure, unduly superstitious, and highly influenced by the imagination' (Menzel 1953: 117), and we have seen enough to know that the tendency remains to interpret meteorological formations and mirages in religious terms. He makes this point clearly by turning to two cases where illusion has persisted in gaining the upper hand, even in the modern period; one is the 1938 broadcast of a dramatization of *The War of the Worlds*, concerning the plausibility of a Martian invasion; the other concerns the origins of a story in 1950 of crashed Venusian space ships and recovered bodies. In these two chapters, Menzel develops his analysis of the roots of superstition in the modern period, identifying a further stage to superstition in the irrational belief in science, and seeking to attribute responsibility for the cultivation and spread of what he terms 'pseudoscience'.

He first recounts Orson Welles' re-telling of H. G. Wells' drama, which Welles transferred to New Jersey with a Princeton astronomer as both expert and narrator, and then turns to Cantril's research (1940) into the causes of the delusions suffered by a part of the listeners as to the reality of what they were hearing. In Menzel's words, 'Ignorance, insecurity, and lack of self-confidence have fostered a tendency towards a blind acceptance of scientific authority that has apparently supplanted the similar faith in medieval demons and sea serpents, witchcraft and sorcery. The radio drama's scientific jargon, endorsed by ostensibly valid scientific authority, precipitated panic among the blind disciples of the "scientific faith"' (Menzel 1953: 142–143). His broader conclusion is that 'modern men, confident that they were successfully practising the methods of science, thus carried germs of an invisible cultural disease – germs of inexperience, insecurity, and irrationality' (Menzel 1953: 143). The broadcast, in short, revealed the potential within the American population, given certain personality types and uncertain political and economic conditions, for a display of mass hysteria, fostered by a 'cultural disease' associated with the advances in scientific understanding.

He offers two ways forward. On the one hand, positively, we might aim to cure this disease by 'a better understanding of science and less emotion in the interpretation of nature' (Menzel 1953: 143). On the other hand, we might seek to attack the roots of this most recent form of superstition. Flying saucers 'possess certain qualities in common' with the Martian incident (Menzel 1953: 144), in that they call upon a widespread myth for which newspapers, journals and books are responsible, creating a 'ceaseless propaganda' shaped by a context – a 'listening situation' (Menzel 1953: 146) – of fears of war and annihilation which make ordinary citizens open to suggestion (Menzel 1953: 145). Again, in short, the newspapers exploit a situation of anxiety which renders the public psychologically vulnerable to some bad ideas. This analysis develops into an attack on the role of the press in promoting 'pseudoscience' and the part played by supposed 'scientific experts'. Keyhoe may be one of the writers he has in mind. He distinguishes between such false experts and true scientists whose reasoning has been shown subsequently to be erroneous, giving the example of Lowell's supposed Martian canal systems. He offers some advice on how to detect the fallacious logic of pseudoscience.

He also appeals to the responsibility of the publishers and hints at the possibility of censorship, for the stakes are high; he cautions against exploiting the American public by 'feeding them fiction in the guise of fact under the protection of a free press' (Menzel 1953: 148), and points out (presumably drawing on the experience of the Washington incident) that, because of these fictions, an enemy attack could readily be mistaken for an invasion from Mars.

Menzel therefore articulates a complete version of the intelligence community's concern with flying saucers (expressed in the Robertson panel report): this is an unhelpful public enthusiasm with security implications because of the potential for mass hysteria, which should be tackled by cultural responses. The form this unhelpful response takes is an uncritical endorsement of pseudoscience, taking us into a world of simulacra and traps for the unwary.

The second case is a further instance of the pseudoscience identified, concerning the origin, acceptance, and persistence of a story about a series of crashed space craft with both the bodies of Venusian spacemen aboard and the capture of live spacemen (Menzel 1953: 154). He has something of a scoop here, having had access to university files on the case, which first appeared in print in Frank Skully's *Behind the Flying Saucers* (1950). I shall not outline the material, which concerns a lecturer visiting the University of Denver to talk about flying saucers. Menzel was particularly exercised by talk of 'machines employ[ing] magnetic lines of force as a source of power and as tracks to guide them through space' and of the crashes being attributed to 'magnetic faults' (Menzel 1953: 154), talk which he analyses in some detail, concluding that the various linked speculations are no more than a play on some scientific jargon, and that the whole is a hoax and a tall tale (Menzel 1953: 159). He then describes the uncritical reception of Skully's book, which both fails to detect the scientific imposture and transmits the tale, as well as mentioning the convictions for fraud of both the lecturer and his expert source (Menzel 1953: 163–164). He concludes with some reflections on the place of academic freedom in the University and the real possibility of its abuse by 'communists and other crackpots in various fields' (Menzel 1953: 166), drawing attention again to the seriousness of the dilemma.

These warnings in turn prepare us for the third thesis, which we might think of as the public understanding of science, focussed in explaining the true causes of the series of astronomical and meteorological phenomena which might be taken for flying saucers. He begins this section with a discussion of the fallacy that 'seeing is believing' (Menzel 1953: 169, 170), for sense impressions inform but do not constitute understanding. The two examples of the 1938 broadcast and the more recent hoax demonstrate the separation between common sense and a scientific understanding, for the senses by themselves are deceptive, and must be supplemented by the right understanding. Understanding is culturally learnt; he gives the example of a man interpreting what he sees from a window as a parade and not an invasion. We have recourse to 'memory of past experience to give meaning to perception', and he adds that 'if we conjure up memories from science fiction for our basis [of understanding], we may accept the space-craft hypothesis' (Menzel 1953: 170).

'Superstition', then, 'results from a misapplication of logic', endowing events with 'totally irrelevant causes'. He makes this account more complex, adding the feature that these irrational explanations are influenced by emotion and, 'in the case of the saucers, the predominant feeling that distorts the understanding is fear, sometimes combined with wishfulness and expectancy' (Menzel 1953: 171). And he sums up as follows: 'problems of understanding the world lie ... in the processes of perception, thinking, and motivation' (Menzel 1953: 172), to which he adds learning. We might wonder how precisely, given this complexity, to distinguish scientific from unscientific accounts and, furthermore, what might cause us to adhere to one rather than the other.

He then runs seriatim through explanations for the various phenomena introduced in the early chapters and in the survey of older materials. He begins with the rainbow, which allows him to discuss questions of distance and situation relative to the observer, leading to the optics of reflected light and 'spectres' in fog. This discussion leads to a range of effects produced by sunlit ice crystals in the atmosphere, including sun-dogs (mock suns) and halos, and reflections from beyond the horizon (including moon-dogs), together with the behaviour of reflections again with respect to the observer, depending on the angle of reflection and the direction of travel with respect to the source. Description of the influence of clouds and variations in temperature, including 'inversions', leads to an account of the lens-like properties of bodies of air, reflecting, dispersing and distorting light, and an account of mirage formation and the behaviour of mirage effects.

Menzel then perhaps diverts into a detailed chapter on the aurora borealis and its relation to solar activity, for few or no saucer phenomena are to be explained by these effects (Menzel 1953: 225), although this excursus allows him to clarify the impossibility of using the magnetic field as a source of vehicular power. He returns to more promising material on comets and meteors although again, after a review of the current science, he concludes that 'since 1947, no one has included a comet as a flying saucer' (Menzel 1953: 248). Meteors or shooting stars however are sighted frequently and may account for the green fireballs seen particularly in the North Mexican desert, owing to the clear atmosphere, which also explains certain properties of the sightings (the appearance of low speed because of the distance over which sighting is possible).

Much from the earlier chapters is pertinent when it comes to considering the evidence from radar (in Menzel's chapter 19), for radar mirages exist under the same conditions as optical mirages and show comparable behaviour: reflections of stable objects may appear to move if the layers of air are moving; objects on the ground may be confused with objects in the air, and near objects with far; and objects may first loom and then disappear. Menzel begins the chapter with the Washington incident, but his best examples of radar mirages are drawn from his experience with the Navy (268) and from North African wartime incidents (Menzel 1953: 269).

Menzel sums up his conclusions in the statement with which we began, that 'All reports of saucers ... result from unusual and unfamiliar conditions in the atmosphere', to which he adds, that these objects have appeared throughout the ages, often causing superstitious fear, and that the present phenomenon is the result of those who exploit the illusion and people's love of 'science fiction stuff' (Menzel 1953: 272).

Perhaps confusingly, he ends with a discussion (originally printed as a stand-alone article) of the prospects of exploring the Moon, Mars and Venus, prefaced with a review of the likelihood of there being other forms of life in the Universe, and the problem of distance between star systems. This discussion is in line however with an earlier comment he makes in passing, to the effect that 'the flying saucers of today have no relationship to the space travel of tomorrow' (Menzel 1953: 146).

Achievements and reputation

What has Menzel achieved? He makes the case for all flying saucer reports being accounted for by natural phenomena of one kind or another. This argument can be extended to cover past instances of sightings, signs and wonders. Such an empirical approach can never, however, be definitively closed, for every interpretation will be haggled over and, more significantly, it is always open to residues of unexplained cases and to the appearance of new evidence.

He bolsters this case with a polemic against the tradition of suspicion of official pronouncements and scientific sources, a tradition which has its origins in primitive belief, but evolves into superstition and then into modern 'pseudoscience'. His initial target is the false experts who spread these pseudoscientific myths, but he extends his criticism to the irresponsibility of publishers who give space to these pronouncements, citing the security implications that might ensue. Indeed, he goes further, fearing that a small, hidden group of cult leaders create the ideas given legitimacy by so-called experts who take advantage of the public's credence in science, and that these ideas, spread for profit by publishers exploiting the freedom of the press, will corrupt American minds, shaped by a distrust of authority and a fear of media manipulation, possibly allowing the destruction of American society in a crisis with Soviet powers. He offers no evidence for this construction.

This is quite a complex message, with a degree of special pleading. Overall, the rejection of the interplanetary hypothesis exists within a framework which resembles that of Keyhoe's advocacy of the same theory: the notion of a hidden elite pulling the levers behind appearances, a conspiracy within orthodox society that is neither sufficiently recognized nor effectively combatted, which threatens dire consequences. In each case, it is not clear exactly who are the conspirators, nor what are their intentions, nor the means used, nor the precise nature of the outcomes to be feared (although the Russians' taking advantage of the situation plays in either case). But both the interplanetary hypothesis and its denial can be construed within this framework, and both appeal to an understanding of the scientific method which looks to eliminate candidates explaining the situation, to leave only one possible account remaining. These are both naturalistic accounts, which will find their object in the world; there is no trace in either of any notion of human participation or construction of the object in question. It may be that a naturalistic approach is part of a conspiratorial mindset.

Menzel published two further books on the topic, both with co-authors (*The World of Flying Saucers*, with Lyle Boyd, 1963, and *The UFO Enigma*, with Ernest Taves, 1977), which did not alter his approach (see also his last article, Menzel 1968, a testimony before a Congressional Enquiry).

He clearly had a peppery and, possibly, a vindictive character (see Clark 1998: 395). His reputation has been subject to revision on three counts; I mention these briefly not to adjudicate but as further indication of the 'unseemly effects' that mark the lives and reputations of those caught up in the flying saucer phenomenon.

The first count revises his relations with the Air Force in the early period, drawing on details of a meeting with Pentagon officials in May 1952 contained in Ruppelt's notes (see Clark 1998: 390; cf. Swords' briefer account – Swords and Powell 2012: 152). Menzel's attitude, his potential interest in being a paid consultant, and his results were commented on sceptically by ATIC (Air Technical Intelligence Center), and this breakdown may in turn be reflected in Menzel's criticisms of Air Force limitations, together with his disguising his outsider status. The second concerns criticism by the scientific community of the abstract nature of his findings, which came to a head in the mid-1960s when an astrophysicist, James McDonald, challenged his work on technical grounds (see Clark 1998: 394; Swords and Powell 2012: 297, 317; Peebles 1994: 172ff.; 184f.).

The third controversy concerned the claim that Menzel belonged to an elite secret research group, 'Operation Majestic-12 (MJ-12)', supposedly set up by presidential executive order in September 1947 to oversee policy and research relating to 'two crashed UFOs and the bodies of four extraterrestrial humanoids' (Clark 1998: 394). The document that revealed the existence of MJ-12 only appeared in December 1984; it has been claimed to offer proof of Menzel's role as an actor in the double plot of government secret knowledge of UFOs on the one hand with the tactic of official denial of the reality of extra-terrestrial life on the other. Peebles devotes some pages (Peebles 1994: 264–268) to exposing the fraudulent nature of the document and its claims, while noting that the forgery continues the theme of 'distrust of "secret societies" as "elitist cabals", a privileged brotherhood counter to American principles' (Peebles 1994: 268).

In sum, for such an actor, little of character, life or work will be left unchallenged; all aspects of personality are caught up in disputes of evaluation and representation within the force field created by flying saucer reports.

III. A shared model of language

Before turning to Keyhoe's reply to this formidable rejection of the interplanetary hypothesis, I want to consider further what the two positions have in common. Both accounts with which we are concerned present themselves as objective descriptions of what is the case, and therefore quickly become drawn into theories as to why these descriptions are rejected by some actors. A positive or negative account of flying saucers as real objects needs to be accompanied by a theory of error; in Keyhoe's case, the need to understand the motives behind the Air Force's supposed prevarications and cover-ups; in Menzel, a narrative of the popular love of tall stories and an uncritical acceptance of pseudoscience as survivals of the primitive mind. Both are versions of what we can call 'the language of science' – an unconscious model of how scientific language works in the world, its virtues, limits, and vulnerability. These are presuppositions or mental habits of some depth which discipline, control and correct both what can be known and what is excluded from knowledge.

By taking this approach (which draws on Jenkins 2013: 68–75), we are not taking the language model on its own terms, as offering a value-free description of the world 'out there', matched by an equally objective psychological account of its reception, but instead supposing that words are used to persuade both the speaker and hearers of some worldview or another, and that language employed in this fashion creates new possibilities rather than simply offering a representation of the world in speech. Description and persuasion are not mutually exclusive activities, they are, rather, mutually implicated.

The question then is, what is this objective or 'scientific' use of language – adopted by both Keyhoe and Menzel – meant to persuade us of? What account of the world does it contain? We should note that we are looking at claims made on behalf of the 'scientific method', rather than offering any account of the practice of scientists when engaged in their work.

The model makes two claims. In the first place, it suggests that words, when used properly, describe what is the case, so that descriptions can correspond unambiguously with the facts. It is possible to get things right. Scientific language has the ambition of describing the world as it is without significant remainder and does not contemplate alternatives. There is little recognition that circumstances may create irresolvable conflicts in which descriptions may participate.

In the second place, this account contains a particular view of what a person is and the place of intentional action. This model of language assumes that only humans are capable of showing intentional agency, and that the rest of the world is made up of things, open to being known but not to undertaking purposeful action. We might refine that account by saying that intentional action is structured by knowledge of the past and hope for the future, while non-human animate things can act only in the present, responding to stimuli, to needs of some kind. Yet, as we know, this account is insufficient for, within the class of persons, the model also distinguishes between truthful and deceptive accounts of motivation, for some people are inwardly committed to truth (or science), while others lack such a commitment. This is where a theory of error becomes necessary.

On this model, scientists speak in the name of science and not on their own behalf, and so the principal problem becomes explaining the motivation of those who speak mistakenly. A scientist can be thought of as a person who notes contradictions and conflicts in evidence and seeks their meaning; he does not seek to rationalize these conflicts or to distract attention from them by displacement activities or made-up narratives.

The initial claim – that scientific language describes the world as completely as possible, without evaluation – then contains a moral demand, that the scientist be sufficiently strong-minded and honest to pursue the truth, at a cost, if necessary, to step beyond the comfort of commonly-held positions and shared opinions of the many. Our examples here are distinctively masculine in their tone and approach, particularly in their treatment of opponents, so it is fair to say of the scientist (in this model) that he lives truthfully, not, however, by any virtue inherent in himself, but so that scientific truth may speak through him. He channels science. He is never alone in doing this; he is supported by adopting the company of others of like mind and by making certain commitments and by following particular methods and disciplines. And by doing so, he serves a higher cause, and his person is doubled in this way.

While scientific language appears to be purely descriptive, then, it also contains a vocation and has a performative aspect. The person who is called, through his scientific commitment, has the task of making himself into someone who understands the world (and himself) scientifically, and then of sharing this scientific point of view, for it contains the secrets of the world's workings. Scientific language not only makes the (scientific) self, but also offers a different future to those who live by other standards, for they too could avoid error, deception, and disappointment, and live according to the truth.

In this fashion, speaking about the world truthfully has the potential to shape the world differently, and to be able to do so demands moral formation. In this account, truth is in principle straightforward; the words of a description correspond to a single meaning and may be understood by their literal reference. In this frame, we work with fixed correspondences and distrust changing forms or fluidity of meaning, and avoid, likewise, the emotions, involuntary solidarities, and loyalty to traditions: everything that clouds the work of charting those correspondences. Becoming a scientist – or, in Keyhoe's case, adopting a scientific attitude – then demands a transformation in the person; using scientific language demands purifying the self of previous habits, understandings and relationships, undertaking an apprenticeship in which one makes scientific speech one's own, adopting the company and instruction of other scientists. And, as one becomes fluent in this form of speech, one gains both a new character and a new authority. Science, as it were, speaks through the scientist and a new set of habits, bodily actions and emotions are introduced: one becomes a person who pays attention to the facts, remains calm in the face of apparent contradiction or frustration, always reasonable and open to correction.

This picture is not, of course, entirely true of either of our figures. The conflict originally encountered in the world, in the struggle between truthful (literal) speech and error, emerges within the scientist, demanding both a vigilant seeking after error in others and also continual monitoring of the self. As Latour (1993) has remarked, the scientist's task is a work of purification, moving away from collective human behaviours and material forms and towards the life of the mind, intentionally motivated and expressed through sincere speech. And through such speech, others can be moved to participate in the truth, breaking old ties and forming new ones, joining in new projects with a salvific horizon, aiming at reforming and indeed saving the world for truth. The whole project presupposes the possibility of 'direct communication' between minds.

In short, although Keyhoe and Menzel present opposed accounts, they share both their presuppositions and the ambition to offer a moral account of the world, a theodicy with its explanation of human woes and offering a clear remedy to those evils. In this ambition and in their ventriloquism of a higher form of life – the life scientific – they resemble some of the other actors who emerge in this history.

IV. Keyhoe's reply: Flying Saucers from Outer Space

Keyhoe's 1950 account was structured around the deciphering of a complex conspiracy on the part of the government and the military to hide the facts and yet simultaneously to prepare the public for the revelation of the truth about interplanetary life. He indeed detailed the features to be expected in investigating this world of official secrets – misleading tips, blind alleys, unexpected assistance, confidential leads, stunning contradictions (Keyhoe 1950b: 15) – all of which he encountered. This perspective of living in a *Noir* film is not lightened in the later books. Nothing could indicate the marriage of noir fiction and public reality in the period better than the reputation Keyhoe enjoyed for sobriety of judgement and reliability as a source. Jung (in a book published in 1958) praises Keyhoe's first two books 'which are based on official material and studiously avoid the wild speculation, naïveté, or prejudice of other publications' (Jung 1978: 6; see also Jung's letter to Keyhoe, Jung 1978: 137–138). And Keyhoe (1953) carries an endorsement from a Pentagon press officer, again praising his qualities as 'a responsible, accurate reporter'. His highly artificial story is taken for granted and read as operating within the rules of common sense in the period.

His second book, *Flying Saucers from Outer Space* (1953), repeats the twofold thesis of the earlier account, claiming that flying saucers are machines from another planet, evidence of a higher civilization observing the earth, and that the controversy around this claim is due to Air Forces tactics: they know the interplanetary hypothesis is true, but fear creating public panic by acknowledging this, for any signs of mass hysteria could be exploited by the Russians in the case of a Soviet attack.

In practice, he takes the interplanetary hypothesis for granted; the story concerns the human response. This is how he introduces an account of the flap leading up to the Washington incident: 'During the first two weeks of July [1952] the saucers' reconnaissance of the earth was rapidly stepped up. Flying singly, in pairs, or in group formations, the strange machines were seen all over the world. But in the early stage there were few public sightings … Most of the saucers were operating at night, and they seemed to be focusing on defense bases, atomic plants, and military planes' (Keyhoe 1953: 54).

The time frame of the book was created by the short period of active cooperation of Project Blue Book with journalists, initiated by Ruppelt after the Washington incident press conference in July 1952 and terminated after the Robertson panel report in January 1953. Keyhoe constructs the narrative around dialogues with three interlocutors, Al Chop, a spokesman from the Pentagon Office of Public Information, 'Jim Riordan' (a pseudonym), a pilot with Korean experience who had just left the service, and Wilbur Smith, an engineer who had overseen the first Canadian saucer project. They each have a role to play: Smith fills out technical details, Riordan offers a pilot's experience both of unidentified flying objects and of the military organization's attitude to such witnesses, while Chop offers a muted commentary on divisions within the Pentagon as the pro-saucer faction's fortune waxed and waned.

The narrative plot repeats the earlier motif of progressive revelation, summed up in this passage:

> Clearly, Intelligence … wanted the public to see this conclusive proof that the saucers were interplanetary machines.
>
> Step by step, they had shown me convincing evidence adding up to this answer …

> First, the simultaneous radar and visual sightings, which proved the saucers were not temperature inversions or optical illusions. Then the Oneida case, official proof of solid objects behind the mysterious lights. After this, case after case with pilots' statements that the saucers were controlled machines, with speeds and maneuvres beyond the power of any earth-made aircraft. Fourth, the Utah pictures [Tremonton], which they had fully confirmed when they could easily have denied their existence. And now this mother-ship report, tying it all together into the space-ship answer. (Keyhoe 1953: 165–166)

In this account, the Air Force, or at least the pro-saucer faction, supports Keyhoe's research and pushes towards his conclusions; he is giving voice to the inside story. Chop's final act as a spokesman is to hand over reports backing up the last stage of the sequence of evidence and to endorse the interplanetary hypothesis: 'You've been right from the very start' (Keyhoe 1953: 248). This endorsement protects Keyhoe's initial thesis intact, despite such a concession as an intelligence officer telling him that the early Project Sign did not hold the interplanetary hypothesis in any form and had quite other (honest) motives for giving no clear answers: they 'were convinced the saucers didn't exist ... and the majority believed each sighting must have a conventional explanation' (Keyhoe 1953: 123). Keyhoe's earlier theme continues regardless: there is a mystery to be resolved, with a technical solution, which has been concealed by official sources for reasons that have to be deciphered.

Because of his sources, he offers a sketch of the political groupings at work in the Pentagon in this brief period in accordance with his thesis:

> It was a curious situation. The officers and civilian officials involved in UFO policy decisions were divided, roughly, into three main groups. The first ... Group A, believed that sighting reports should be made public to prepare the country for the final solution – whatever it proved to be. Most of the men in this group had seen all the evidence and were convinced the saucers are machines superior to any known aircraft. The other two groups believed in silence, but for different reasons. Those in the B group also had seen the evidence, believed the saucers were real, but feared the effects of a public admission. Group C was made up of hardheaded nonbelievers. Most of them had never troubled to examine the ATIC [Air Technical Intelligence Center] evidence; the few who had, flatly refused to believe it. (Keyhoe 1953: 122–123)

By the last chapter, the anti-saucer faction has gained the upper hand, while the press officer, as a parting gesture, gives Keyhoe the permissions he needs to publish his account of the reports used and hints at a classified meeting leading to a secret report, for which he cannot give out the conclusions. This reversal shapes Keyhoe's increasingly antagonistic subsequent relationship with the Air Force, worked out through NICAP (National Investigations Committee on Aerial Phenomena). The optic employed never alters.

The book develops two themes introduced in 1950, based in part on access to some forty recent Air Force reports (see Keyhoe 1953, Appendix II): it offers more a detailed classification of spaceship types (Keyhoe 1953: 156), as well as further discussion of electromagnetic fields of force as a possible means of saucer propulsion (Keyhoe 1953: 131–144), including evidence for action at a distance on aeroplanes that draw too close (Keyhoe 1953: 139). The second topic indeed gives a clue to the book's probable main purpose, which is to discredit Menzel's arguments against the existence of flying saucers, for Menzel was also dismissive of theories of propulsion drawing on magnetic lines of force.

This objective is clear from the first chapter, which is organized around a refutation of Menzel's theories, given particularly the recourse to temperature inversions to explain the Washington incident, for that incident is the event motivating Keyhoe's second book, including the reversal of Air Force policy, access to reports, endorsement and so forth. The chapter first establishes Keyhoe's new 'insider' status with respect to the Pentagon and, as part of this, Chop, a 'civilian expert on UFOs' (Keyhoe 1953: 3), passes him not only a set of recent Intelligence reports of sightings but also 'an ATIC statement bluntly refuting the theories of Dr Donald Menzel, a Harvard astronomer who had tried to debunk the saucers as mirages and other illusions' (Keyhoe 1953: 5). Riordan also mocks the dismissal of experienced witnesses' sightings in this fashion (Keyhoe 1953: 11).

Keyhoe's case against Menzel evolves over the period under consideration: the theory of 'temperature-inversion' serves as the 'one loophole' available to General Samford after the Washington incident, yet Menzel's theories quickly become an obstacle to the hoped-for acceptance of evidence for flying saucers (Keyhoe 1953: 89), and then become a target for those in the Pentagon who wish to air the interplanetary hypothesis (Keyhoe 1953: 102, 109). Keyhoe sums up his position: 'At this time [July 1952], by sheer good luck, I had gone to the Pentagon and made my offer [to cooperate with the Air Force if given the whole picture]. By then the Menzel theory had served its purpose; some Intelligence officers felt it should not be allowed to stand as the official answer. Believing that I would give a fair picture of the Air Force problem, Intelligence had released the facts which wrecked the inversion story' (Keyhoe 1953: 125).

And what is the 'Air Force problem'? Menzel and others, by their expert scepticism, 'were pushing the Air Force into a tight corner. Each time ... [in offering a sceptical explanation] the Air Force had to say publicly what the saucers are *not*. Each time it was pushed closer to the fateful admission of what the saucers are'. Yet the Pentagon did not want to make this admission until they had 'absolute proof that the saucers were not hostile' (Keyhoe 1953: 15).

In this fashion, Keyhoe incorporates Menzel in that part of his thesis concerning the vacillations of Air Force intentions while, at the same time, discrediting Menzel's challenge to the interplanetary hypothesis by relaying Air Force opinion concerning the invalidity of his theories. A major part of the motivation of the 1953 essay is to put Menzel down.

NICAP

Once the Air Force adopted a settled anti-saucer stance after the Robertson panel report in 1953, Keyhoe hardened his position, forming a campaign to force the Air Force to make its reports public, with the aim, based on these records, of simultaneously establishing the interplanetary hypothesis beyond doubt and exposing previous official evasions and duplicity. The titles of his two subsequent books – *The Flying Saucer Conspiracy* (1955) and *Flying Saucers: Top Secret* (1960) – show the direction of travel,[5] and to this end, he helped form and then took over NICAP (the National Investigations Committee on Aerial Phenomena), using both the newsletter (the *UFO Investigator*) and the organization to lobby for a Congressional investigation of Air Force records.[6]

This later period continues the earlier themes without major developments; I shall rely on Peebles (1994) to offer a summary.[7] Peebles identifies a series of topics.

First, Keyhoe built the target of Air Force secrecy by identifying two recent military orders, JANAP 146 and AFR 200-2, conceived as aimed respectively at keeping UFO reporting by pilots secret and confining their investigation to three secret groups within the Air Force (see Keyhoe 1955). He portrayed these initiatives as concealing new encounters, at the same time identifying a high level 'silence group' who lay behind them, tightening censorship within the Armed Forces (Peebles 1994: 112).

The second topic concerns the formation of civilian flying saucer groups, in the context of the Robertson panel recommendations, although not a direct consequence of the Report. These groups monitored sightings and pressed the Air Force to release their records, something they refused to do, both on the grounds of concealing intelligence procedures and with the aim of discouraging interest in flying saucers. This refusal fed into theories of a conspiracy and confirmed the assumption that the files contained proof of the interplanetary theory (Peebles 1994: 111).

---

5   His last – *Aliens from Space* (Keyhoe 1973) – lacks the animus of the earlier books.
6   We return to materials touched on in the third essay, *Martian Linguistics*, from the Air Force point of view, now considering the ufologists' perspective.
7   Peebles draws on Jacobs (1975) for the skeleton of his account of NICAP, supplementing that record with documents that have become available later. It is worth remarking that Peebles, who is a sceptic concerning what he calls 'the flying saucer myth', is not cited by other historians of the movement such as Clark (1998) or Swords (in Swords and Powell 2012), who readily acknowledge Jacobs' pioneering role; none of Clark, Swords or Jacobs count as sceptics, while each is a careful historian. Yet, as far as I can judge, Peebles is their equal both in accuracy and the meticulous handling of sources, and he offers the most detailed account of NICAP's history; the divide is on ideological grounds alone.

Third, Peebles traces the history of one of these groups, the Flying Saucer Discussion Group, started in Washington DC in Spring 1956, animated by Clara John, whom we shall meet again as editor of George Adamski's claim of a first contact with a pilot from a flying saucer, and by Townsend Brown, an inventor who sought government funding for 'an electric space propulsion system that worked on antigravity' (Peebles 1994: 114). This group saw the need for an umbrella organization to co-ordinate investigation both of aerial phenomena (UFOs) and of the possibilities of (human) space flight; this proposal led to the incorporation of NICAP in August 1956.

Keyhoe helped Brown assemble a board including ex-forces officers, physicists, ministers and businessmen, and then with their help took over as director from Brown in January 1957. Keyhoe published a proposal in the first issue of the *UFO Investigator* (July 1957) that NICAP become an officially recognized guide and advisor to the Air Force, its interlocutor with the public and arbiter between the military and the public on matters concerning flying saucers. Peebles sums up the conflicting assumptions of the two parties: 'NICAP believed the Air Force had proof UFOs were real and all its efforts were aimed at forcing an admission. The Air Force took the narrow view that UFO publicity was the direct cause of sightings. Therefore, efforts were made to solve sightings and minimize publicity' (Peebles 1994: 117).

In retrospect, the noir plot, deriving from war comics and the business of reading of all the evidence according to the given narrative, assembling disparate elements to form a coherent incident with anomalies ignored and sometimes introducing fictional ideas as part of the construction, seems too far-fetched to be plausible. Yet, at the time, Keyhoe's account, with the two linked assertions of the interplanetary hypothesis and state concealment of its proofs, was not only regarded as plausible but taken for granted by many actors, and the convincing nature of the narrative generated a range of effects.

On the one hand, this 'common sense' element is demonstrated as NICAP sought to form and lead the civilian UFO organizations, using the notion of direct human contact with beings from interplanetary craft as a boundary marker, expelling those who claimed contact as a means of sorting acceptable from unacceptable beliefs. There then were reasonable and unreasonable positions within the bounds of the interplanetary hypothesis, to be made operational by membership. This attitude allowed, for example, a provisional alliance with the APRO (Aerial Phenomena Research Organization, founded in 1952) which, although it allowed reports of landings and sightings of UFO pilots – both of which NICAP did not – drew the line at contactees (Peebles 1994: 141). The strictness of internal discriminations matched the requirements for overcoming a total external conspiracy.

On the other hand, the organization gained a hearing in its lobbying for Congressional hearings, conceived as the best means of forcing the Air Force's hand and making them publish the reports they held and the records of their evasions and concealments to date. In Peebles' account, NICAP came closest to obtaining Congressional hearings on UFOs in 1957–1958, being frustrated when the Air Force convinced the relevant committee chairman to drop the issue (Peebles 1994: 128–131). Keyhoe gives an account of this period of hope followed by disappointment in *Flying Saucers: Top Secret* (1960), repeating the pattern of the 1953 book. NICAP returned to the charge in 1960–1962, when again Congress showed interest in UFOs, this time also expressing dissatisfaction with Air Force openness on the topic (Peebles 1994: 136). Keyhoe's published aims were, as before, to hold the Air Force to account and to place NICAP in a role supervising the release of restricted information to the public. ATIC counter-briefed, and the prospect of hearings retreated, the Congressional chairman in this instance denouncing Keyhoe's attempt to ' "be-little", "defame", and "ridicule" the Air Force' (Peebles 1994: 158). NICAP also returned to campaign for Congressional hearings in 1965–1966, in the context of an upturn in reported UFO sightings (Peebles 1994: 153–154). In short, the interplanetary hypothesis, to which Keyhoe had helped give shape fifteen years before, while not subject to any consensus, dominated the terms of the public debate, including the press and the national political level.

At the same time as failing in attempts to force the Air Force to confirm their thesis, NICAP also failed in uniting the ufological camp. There were financial problems, the result of maintaining a Washington office for lobbying purposes (Peebles 1994: 136), and in July 1952, APRO denounced NICAP as a lobby group uselessly attacking the Air Force (Peebles 1994: 141); they wished to focus on reports of sightings. Both NICAP and APRO declined by the end of the 1960s. Keyhoe was deposed as director of NICAP by the board at the end of 1969; Peebles reports that financial mismanagement was the presenting cause, but that the membership had tired of Keyhoe's obsession with the Air Force cover-up. APRO was hit by a defection of members in 1969 who went on to found the Mutual UFO Network (MUFON).

The period saw a changing of the guard. The Center for UFO Studies (CUFOS), led by Alan Hynek, was founded in 1974, and a counter-organization, the Committee for the Scientific Investigation of Claims of the Paranormal (CISCOP), in 1976. During the build-up to the Condon Report (1968), a new advocate of what had become the Extra-Terrestrial Hypothesis emerged to replace Keyhoe – James McDonald – as well as a replacement for Menzel in Philip Klass, later a prominent member of CISCOP (Peebles 1994: 172ff.). In Peebles' account, these various changes signal the shattering of what he calls the flying saucer myth, which then took a decade to reassemble (Peebles 1994: 194); he identifies three new themes – cattle mutilations, alien abductions, and crashed saucers – which combined by the early 1990s into the alien myth (Peebles 1994: 213).

Concluding remarks

Keyhoe and Menzel defined a framework, differing only between advocacy and scepticism, which set the terms of the debate which endured for a long while and, indeed, has not yet disappeared from the basic reporting mindset. They consolidated a local version of the alternatives of 'truth or error', only turning to the imagination, in the form of a love of fiction, to explain choices made between this pair. We can call attention to several features of this frame.

First, Keyhoe was utterly dependent on Air Force materials; without their work, there would have been no interplanetary hypothesis to promote. It was no different in Menzel's case, although he took an opposing view on many details. Despite appearances, and a good deal of criticism that each offers of Air Force procedures and practices, both were underlabourers in an Air Force field.

Second, there are parallels between Keyhoe's and Menzel's careers with regard to flying saucers, despite differences in background and education. These include changes in life opportunities, means of gaining income, company kept and employment of time, particularly in Keyhoe's case, but not negligible in Menzel's. And, despite surface differences, there are clearly similar patterns of thought at work in each.

With respect to these patterns of thought, we should note the complex constructions needed either to be able to claim the truth of sightings or to deny them. The presuppositions of the language model being invoked control all the possible disputes, coming down to an advocacy of realism and a rejection of the powers of the imagination. But in each case, advocacy and rejection are mixed and so presented with no great conviction. The realism of the truth claims is muted, we might say, and denial of these claims involves a good deal of work on the powers of the imagination.

And last, the conflicts and intractable misunderstandings that characterize these life trajectories and thought patterns have had widespread influence, catching up a wide range of serious people in different professions and with degrees of public exposure: state employees, the military, scientists, journalists and politicians and, focus of the next chapter, members of the public.

CHAPTER 2

George Adamski: A life

We now turn to a man who, rather than resisting the possibilities offered by shifts in categories and the emergence of new objects, embraced them. When they make an appearance, new things do not need to be impoverished and classified to be understood, but instead, using the resources of narrative forms, may be put to work imaginatively, telling stories that express and explore the new forms, new collective ways of thought and living. In this fashion, fictions not only reflect change but also alter the potential of social life.

This chapter consists of two parts: an investigation of George Adamski's life and contribution and a discussion of what conclusions may be drawn from this description. Adamski serves as a valuable case study, for the abundant materials available allow us to map in detail the sources and processes which are found in many small groups dedicated to awaiting the arrival of visitors from space. His case is exemplary and was also a direct influence on many later groups. In the last two sections, I investigate the mental categories and operational features of small-scale organizations that structure the materials. This more abstract description draws out the opportunities and disturbances that flying saucers brought to interpersonal relationships, innovations and conflicts, opportunities and disturbances that can only be glimpsed in documents available from large-scale organizations such as the military or the space industry. These potentials are given clear expression at the lesser scale and allow insight into the kind of phenomena found when considering the full range of encounters of ordinary citizens with flying saucers.

I. Setting the scene

George Adamski (1891–1965) was the first person to claim contact with a being from a flying saucer, in a meeting in the Californian desert on 20 November 1952. His written-up account was appended to an already completed manuscript by a British author, Desmond Leslie, and published as *Flying Saucers have landed* in September 1953, which is reputed to have sold more than 100,000 copies (Peebles 1994: 96). Adamski published a second book, *Inside the Space Ships*, in 1955, in which he reported travelling in spaceships, viewing other planets in the solar system, and having conversations with spacemen from Venus, Mars and Saturn, who instructed him in their philosophy. A third book followed in 1961. As well as writing, he also produced other evidence of encounter: photographs and films of spaceships, and artefacts marked by spacemen's hieroglyphics.

These accounts and materials gained notice but were contested from the start; Keyhoe, for example, finds the initial report of Adamski's first encounter (reported in the *Phoenix Gazette*, 24 November 1952) worth discussing, although he adopts a sceptical tone (Keyhoe 1953: 158–159), and Adamski gained critics as well as followers in many countries. There is indeed a good deal of material considering his claims, for and against. Other claims of contact followed, so that contactees form part of the spectrum of effects attributable to Air Force investigations into flying saucer reports and lead us towards what we might call the ordinary person's experience of flying saucers. For, if we move away from Keyhoe's security-focussed Washington-military world and Menzel's educated scepticism, it seems reasonable from the non-specialist's point of view to suppose that, if there are interplanetary spacecraft monitoring human activities, they might communicate with humankind to explain their interest and intentions and even land to make contact. This indeed is the plot of the film *The Day the Earth Stood Still* (1951); contact is an extrapolation of elements present in the interplanetary hypothesis, a narrative that made sense to the press and its readers and to Hollywood and its audiences, although it tests that narrative to the limits of its plausibility. We are shifting focus, then, to a series of human events and group encounters and their interactions with the science fiction milieu, on the one hand, and the constellation of military and technical interests, on the other. Two interesting features emerge if we consider Adamski's writings and history. The first is confirmation that the source of ideas about beings from other planets and long-existing travel between planets – the notion that the Earth is part of a wider network of communication, monitoring and visits – is Theosophy, even if in a popularized form.[1] An investigation into Adamski's writings and history supports the claim that Theosophy provided the ideas that shaped his and his readers' notions of life in space, to the extent that other sources of ideas of 'life on other worlds' or 'extraterrestrial life' can probably be discounted: notions of life elsewhere, interplanetary craft, civilizations far in advance of our own, observers monitoring and shaping our development like parents are passed through the lens of theosophical speculation which assembles and focusses these themes. Contemporary accounts of life elsewhere owed their grammar and their sense of possibility to Theosophy. Planetary Spirits become Space Masters (cf. Partridge 2003; Roth 2005; Rothstein 2013).

The second feature concerns the small-group life and social dynamics which are necessary for such ideas to be developed, which are applied to new situations by absorbing contemporary elements, and which find form with sufficient plausibility to spread through the wider society. In that wider setting, these claims are not necessarily accepted as truthful but serve as unofficial accounts which at least merit a hearing, and which, because of that plausibility, provoke the kind of reactions we have seen exemplified in Menzel's contempt for 'pseudoscience' and Keyhoe's rejection of contactees' claims while defending the interplanetary hypothesis.

In Adamski, then, we find a life constructed through an engagement with Theosophy, one that was translated in the period into contact with spacemen in a form that found widespread acknowledgement. A certain amount of work and imagination is needed to reconstruct this aspect

---

1   The claim concerning Theosophy is substantiated in the second essay, *Religion and Science Fiction*.

of the period and its categories. It represents an autodidact theodicy, offering a sense of hope and purpose to parts of a population made up of energetic and intelligent people drawn from anywhere, a population with daily experience of advanced technology, gained from employment, industry, military service, media outlets and observing planes in the sky, who were seeking forms of common moral enterprise in the midst of a conviction both of America's great political power and also obscure threats, internal and external, to security, and without any hegemonic cultural institutions to impose limits to speculation and plausibility (cf. Lepselter 2016).

Deciphering mysteries

Adamski's brief report of first encounter is only forty-eight pages, but it is carefully constructed. In the first chapter, he sets up the possibility of an encounter through a series of episodes, introduces the wider context, says something about himself as the main protagonist, and adds some theosophical grace notes, preparing for the account of the meeting in the second chapter. We will look at these elements in turn. The narrative setting up the possibility of encounter resembles a film treatment or a short story; we have no pretence of separating fictional tropes from contemporary history. The story unfolds progressively and coincidences mount, revealing significant purpose over time. The reader is led into a different understanding of the world and its potential.

Adamski worked in 'Palomar Gardens' on the southern slope of Mount Palomar in California, situated close to the Hale Observatory, which then housed the world's biggest telescope. Palomar Gardens was a property owned by a friend, Alice Wells, and included a café, which provided a location allowing the easy introduction and departure of the various actors – witnesses, interlocutors, mysterious authority figures and so forth – involved in creating the story. Adamski lived in the complex, where he pursued a longstanding interest in 'skywatching and telescopic photography'. He disclaimed any connection with the Observatory nearby (journalists sometimes made this mistake), but made his technical knowledge clear, identifying the types of telescopes he used and naming one of the manufacturers (Leslie and Adamski 1953: 176).[2]

We are then introduced to a series of sightings of 'saucers', which establishes the dimensions of the problem. Adamski's first sighting was of a large black object shaped like a giant dirigible, observed while watching a meteor shower in the company of friends on the night of 9 October 1946. It stood motionless and then shot upwards into space, leaving a trail behind. His first assumption was that this was a new kind of aircraft, developed during the War, now being used to observe the falling meteors at high altitude. However, later that evening the group of observers heard on a radio broadcast that 'a large cigar-shaped space ship' had been observed over San Diego during the meteor shower and reported by hundreds of witnesses. Adamski refused to accept the reports at face value for, as an experienced observer, he knew the distances between Earth and other planets and the speeds achieved by human machines, and so dismissed the claims on the grounds of the time interplanetary travel would take – 'impossible in any human life-span' – and the 'pressures a human body can endure' (Leslie and Adamski 1953: 177). But his scepticism was challenged in the café by six military officers who, while claiming to know something of these matters, refused to go further other than saying the ship in question 'was not of this world' (Leslie and Adamski 1953: 178). This first episode begins to set the scene, introducing the cautious, scientifically minded investigator and his companions, a public united by the media, ready uncritically to credit the existence of flying saucers, and the authoritative military figures who know more than they are willing to say and who, against one's first expectations, support a version of the public interpretation against Adamski's informed scepticism. We might note that authority – being in the know – is more important in this post-War environment than thinking along scientific lines in evaluating the evidence, and Adamski can share in this authority only because he is prepared to change his mind in accordance with the hints he is given. Secret knowledge allows the investigator to go beyond first appearances.

2 Accessed on the SCRIBD website.

Adamski also introduced a further element for, although at this time he believed interplanetary travel to be impossible, he nevertheless believed 'that other planets are inhabited ... [picturing] them as "class rooms" for our experience and development; as the "many mansions" of the vast universe' (Leslie and Adamski 1953: 175). These are theosophical views, cast in a Christian idiom.

Impressed by the officers' intervention, Adamski continued his observations. Discussion of flying saucers increased during the summer of 1947,[3] and his watching was rewarded in August by a second sighting, seeing a series of bright lights, one of which 'stopped in midspace and reversed its path of travel' (Leslie and Adamski 1953: 178). Together with some friends, he counted squadrons of lights crossing the sky, with leaders apparently signalling to those following by reversing direction. Some banked and changed direction, allowing their shape to be observed – 'a ring around a central body, or dome'. The last light to pass paused 'for several seconds in midspace and shot out two powerful beams of light – one towards the south ... the other north ...', before continuing its way. Adamski's previous role as sceptic was taken over by a young man living on the property who could testify to having seen the swarm the previous night but who suspected he had seen 'government experimental aircraft' (Leslie and Adamski 1953: 179). This opinion however was once again contradicted, this time by two scientists from the Observatory in the café, who clearly knew a good deal about the phenomenon but revealed little except to say that 'all the indications pointed to them being interplanetary, because they did not belong to the government'. Adamski had already moved to the position of recognizing the first light, which had reversed direction, 'must be what they call a flying saucer' (Leslie and Adamski 1953: 178). This episode contributes to the building mystery, developing a puzzle to be solved, with the most likely theories being disposed of one by one by well-placed sources.

We jump two years, to late 1949, for the third incident. Once again, the initiative lay in the hands of people from the military industrial complex, who this time recruited Adamski to help their work. Adamski fell into conversation in the café with four men working in Naval electronics

---

[3] It was then that the term emerged.

laboratories, who asked him to take photographs with his telescope of any 'strange craft moving through space', adding they were going to the Observatory to ask for the same co-operation. They discussed the likelihood of the moon having bases for interplanetary craft (Leslie and Adamski 1953: 180). Shortly after this meeting, Adamski took 'two good pictures of an object moving through space ... [while] observing the moon' through his 6–inch telescope. When one of the naval engineers returned to the café, Adamski handed over the photographs, to be passed on to another of the officers in the laboratory.

There is an additional incident nested within this part of the story. While the engineer was making his second visit, they both listened on the café radio to a report of a flying saucer landing in New Mexico. Adamski then gives a brief history of this report. First, the engineer commented at the time that there was more to the incident than the report contained, showing himself to be a man with inside information. Then, Adamski says, the report was later denied, and the incident attributed to an American test missile going out of control. And last, this second story turned out to be a cover-up: a spaceship had landed, as reported, but the government had spread the second story to prevent panic; Adamski only heard this last version in 1951, from some 'government men'.

This is an exemplary sequence of naïve but accurate reporting, a subsequent government cover-up, and the apparently chance revealing of the truth to an interested party who is paying attention. Because of this sequence, the initial incident is reintroduced as a problem needing further interpretation. The person who deciphers the truth behind the sequence of reports is always late on the scene, in the sense either of being absent from the original incident or, if a witness, unaware of what he has seen; the incident cannot be read correctly at sight, but only made sense of retrospectively, through a kind of intelligence work. All sorts of factors are involved in this unlikely series of improbable events which allow the investigator to understand, with hindsight, first the incident, then the deliberate deception, and finally the betrayal of the secret of the conspiracy, with engineers working in new technologies and security operatives playing most of the major roles, and the public and the press taking walk-on parts. The series also serves to redefine Adamski's role as he took on the authority of the engineers and the security men; through no volition of his own other than a scientific attention to the facts he moved from being a bystander like us, in a world we might recognize, to being a player in a world of secrets and significant encounters.

The two photographs brought Adamski to public notice, for a journalist learnt of their existence and, having interviewed Adamski, followed up with an enquiry to the Naval laboratory which, however, denied having received them. He then made further enquiry to the Air Force in Washington, who likewise denied any knowledge of the photographs and stated they did not 'subscribe to the theory that flying saucers were interplanetary missiles' (Leslie and Adamski 1953: 182). Adamski nevertheless continued to pass on any photographic evidence he took to the Air Force, who never made any acknowledgement. Through this press attention he had become, like Keyhoe, a well-intentioned aide to the military, co-operating with and respected by individual members of the establishment, but not recognized by the institution. And, like Keyhoe, he appeared to know a good deal more than the institution was prepared to admit to publicly. Adamski had two articles with his photographs included published in *Fate* magazine (editor Ray Palmer) in 1950 and the following year (Weekley and Adamski 1950; Adamski 1951).

Space craft and the political context

So far, Adamski has set the scene and introduced the main human players – military engineers, the defence establishment, the occasional civilian scientist from the Observatory, members of the public who report sightings, journalists who investigate, and himself, representative of a small group of dedicated enquirers. We have not yet been given any hint that the last named may have been chosen in some way by the non-human objects of their attention. At the same time, he has constructed a recognizable narrative, using a sequence of flashbacks to introduce two intertwined but distinct mysteries. These mysteries concern, on the one hand, a series of sightings of interplanetary craft, the flying saucers, and, on the other, the manipulation of information concerning these sightings by the military and governmental interests. We have met this form before, in Keyhoe, of waking up to the existence of secrets in the world, and of having to distinguish between the hidden control of common-sense perceptions and the non-obvious (and yet in plain sight) events from which attention is being distracted. In the present case, while the concealment is attributed to human causes, the non-obvious events are not, or are suspected not to be. And we find a cast of characters needed both to generate and decipher these secrets: the bland denials issued from high up in the military, together with – later – the security men who utter veiled threats (thereby confirming the existence of secrets they seek to deny) and, on the other side, the experts who drop hints and, by their silences as much as by their words, confirm the intuitions of the investigator. It is worth remarking that everyone in the story is part of larger, if only vaguely defined, groups; the investigator is one of a group of allies (whom we meet in more detail later), and both the dark and the light figures (broadly, security men and engineers respectively) are members of wider collective enterprises. It is a convention that we never get to overhear the meetings of these wider groups where authoritative information is shared or when decisions are made to manipulate the public to protect them, nor do we discover the means adopted or the evidence cited; the meetings can only be inferred from their supposed consequences by individual witnesses.

Adamski then turns to these hidden matters of means and inference, at least in outline, focussing first on the craft themselves and their technical properties, and then on the possible motivations of the actors, which in turn explain the reception given to his reports. He shares a good many concerns in these regards with Keyhoe (1950b). Adamski continued to monitor and photograph the craft, 'white spots far out in space' (Leslie and Adamski 1953: 183), being convinced that they were 'intelligently controlled', yet too distant to be man-made. By the end of 1951, he was convinced the spacecraft were increasing in number and moving closer to Earth, probably for purposes of observation, and allowing him to take better photographs (Leslie and Adamski 1953: 184). He disposed of two theories of their being of human origin, pointing out that no foreign power would test experimental aircraft over another nation's territory and that, if they were American military secret projects, the Air Force would have insisted he stop photographing them (Leslie and Adamski 1953: 184–185). He also speculated that their appearance in the Mount Palomar area was due to their using lines of magnetic force as an energy source, for Mount Palomar lies between two natural magnetic vortices (Leslie and Adamski 1953: 187).

This last line of argument allows him to widen his perspective to include consideration of the Cold War context. For space flight and antigravity propulsion will be a matter of keen interest to both the Pentagon and its enemy (whom he does not name), and because of this interest, the mystery of the spaceships poses a further dilemma. If we were to discover the saucers' source of power, the present economic basis of our civilization would be overturned; furthermore, he believed that progress was being made in this direction and that there were entrenched interests in preventing these developments (Leslie and Adamski 1953: 188). Adamski therefore extends the problem of public deception beyond the (largely benevolent) security organizations to include some ill-defined capitalist interests. Americans are confronted not simply by an external enemy (Russians, aided by deported German scientists), and the well-intentioned interventions of their own security apparatus, but also by an enemy within. This is full-scale paranoia. In this context, he suggests, attempts to undermine his testimony and discredit his evidence become entirely understandable (Leslie and Adamski 1953: 188–189). More optimistically, employing some motifs from Keyhoe, he looks forward to the opening of Air Force files and puts his hope in the perspicacity and honesty of laymen like himself.

This account presents the setting for the encounter in the desert; the spaceships coming closer, with their potential for upending our human and scientific understandings, together with the industrial and economic stakes in play, explaining the motives of those who seek to silence or discredit the reports.

I mentioned theosophical grace notes, and in passing we registered Adamski's belief that the planets were classrooms for our development and experience, gained in past and future lives. He also referred briefly to his personal history as a 'teacher as well as a student of philosophy, seeking an ever-greater understanding of the Laws of the Universe' (Leslie and Adamski 1953: 180), as he elaborated his idea that planets are 'inhabited by beings very much like ourselves – probably different mostly in stages of development only'. Combining this perspective with his practical observations, he concluded that 'with a more scientifically-advanced people on other planets, interplanetary travel was definitely within the realms of possibility'. We might wonder whether his early expression of scepticism might have been only one aspect of his thought. Certainly, the theosophical side of his thinking emerges more clearly when we consider his history and that of the companions who accompanied him into the desert, a group who, like him, were 'hoping to make personal contact and to learn just what these space people looked like and what their purpose was in coming Earthwards …' (Leslie and Adamski 1953: 189).

II. The role of networks and ideas in Adamski's formation

Having established his credentials and his anomalous place among those engaged in monitoring interplanetary approaches to Earth, Adamski briefly introduces his companions on this first 'contact with a man from another world' (Leslie and Adamski 1953: 189), who were to act as witnesses to support his claims. There was, first, a married couple, Al and Betty Bailey, from Winslow, Arizona, who had come to the café in August 1952 and introduced themselves as sharing a keen interest in flying saucers. They had in turn brought along a second couple, Betty and George H. Williamson, from Prescott, Arizona; the four had stayed at Palomar Gardens for several days and had asked to be included in any trips made out into the desert attempting to establish contact. The other two companions were longer-term friends of Adamski, Alice Wells, the owner of the café, and Lucy McGinnis, who acted as Adamski's secretary (Leslie and Adamski 1953: 190). To discover their relationships and the motivations that drew them together on this project, we need to sketch Adamski's history; I have used Hallet (2015).[4]

---

4 I have read several books on Adamski but cite only two – Hallet (2015) and Zinsstag and Good (1983) – preferring to work for the most part with primary texts. Hallet's

Adamski was born in Poland in 1891 and came to the US with his parents in 1893, growing up in up-state New York. He served in the Army from 1913 to 1916, followed by a series of unskilled manual jobs all over the western states, and first came to notice as offering informal philosophy lectures in California in 1926 (the source is an FBI memorandum from December 1953, reproduced in an appendix to Hallet 2015: 194). He married in 1917.[5] Some information on Adamski's lecturing emerges from three newspaper articles from 1933 to 1934 (also reproduced in Hallet), when the couple had moved to Laguna Beach, California. Adamski was named in a report of 17 November 1933 in the *South Coast News* as the agent in the purchase of a property which was to serve as the American headquarters of a movement called 'The Royal Order of Tibet' (which was said to be based in London). He was given the title 'Professor' and reported as at present giving lectures at the Little White Church in Laguna, a church associated with the Order of Loving Service, led by a Mrs Lalita Johnson (of whom more below), and he was to give the first lectures at the new headquarters, which was intended as a monastery, and then to conduct closed classes. A second article of 26 January 1934 reported the opening of the headquarters, with a talk by Adamski on 'Universal Brotherhood'.

An article in the *Los Angeles Times* of 8 April 1934 gives more detail on The Royal Order of Tibet's project. It was to establish the first Tibetan monastery in America, to teach and spread 'the ancient truths' and to create the facilities for teaching, lectures and performances (resembling the theosophists' Point Loma settlement, founded in 1900 by Katherine Tingley – see Ashcraft 2002). Adamski was spokesman for the Order; he is attributed an Egyptian mother and a childhood spent in Tibetan monasteries, learning 'the laws of the lamas' (Hallet notes this is a motif

---

book, originally published in 1983, is valuable because of his collecting and reproducing evidence – newspaper reports, FBI documents, Adamski's photographs, and interviews with participants in the story. While it needs to be treated with caution, for Hallet is late on the scene and has an agenda – he denounces Adamski as a fraud – it is nonetheless a scholarly account.

5   His wife died in 1954; she is absent from witness accounts of the flying saucer period.

borrowed from *The Unknown Life of Jesus Christ* by Nicholas Notovitch (1894) – Hallet 2015: 10). He distinguished sharply between the present aims of the project and the sources it draws on: the intention is to bring out 'the scientific portions of the [ancient] religion' while discarding its 'weird rites and bestial superstitions'. This distinction allows what he referred to as 'the trick of applying age-old knowledge to daily life, to cure the body and mind and to win mastery over self and soul'. He also offered certain clarifications, presumably of a reassuring kind: The Order acknowledges God and Christ, and holds to the basic thought of Hinduism, Buddhism and Christianity, to which it adds the ancient law of Tibet, but its object is 'to put Christianity into everyday use', on the model of 'Christian Science, mental science and other crystallizations of thought'. He also distinguished the discipline demanded by Tibetan Buddhism from the voluntary practices of self-formation now being offered; the institution is intended as a school with a resident community, but with many home students as well.

Having read the *Los Angeles Times* article, Alice Wells (born 1900) contacted Adamski and moved to the Order's house; she remained Adamski's follower and supporter until her death in 1980, continuing his work after his death in 1965. This support was crucial in several respects, not least in publishing; Adamski's long career as a writer began in this period, and he always used an amanuensis; Alice Wells may have been the first of these. He published a series of pamphlets under the imprint of the Royal Order of Tibet: *Wisdom of the Masters of the Far East – Questions and Answers* (1936), *Satan, Man of the Hour* (1937 – a 'philosophical parable', in Hallet's words), *The Kingdom of Heaven on Earth* ('a short philosophical text'), and a book of poems, *Petals of Life* (both also 1937).

Maud Lalita Johnson also published under the same imprint. Johnson (1875–1943) had founded the Order of Loving Service in Laguna, dedicated to the teachings of Baba Premanand Bhavati. Bhavati (died 1914) was a follower of the Krishna Consciousness movement (see Sardella 2013) who had attended the Parliament of Religions in Chicago in 1893 and had remained in the States, teaching in Los Angeles from 1902. The Order of Loving Service had published Johnson's *Square*, dedicated to Bhavati's memory, in 1934, and in 1937, in association with the Royal Order of Tibet, published her *Transmitted Light – Latoo the Instrument, Lalita the Recorder* which, as the title suggests, was a spirit communication transcribed through Johnson's mediumship.[6]

Hallet's view is that Johnson provided the backing for the Royal Order of Tibet's purchase of its headquarters (Hallet 2015: 16). He also suggests Johnson may have been Adamski's teacher; in Adamski's files there was a copy of Johnson's *The Sacred Symbol* (n.d., the same publisher as *Transmitted Light*), another spirit communication, this time from 'a being called Celestor who had lived for half a million years in the 116th plane and has manifested at different times on Venus, Mars, and other planets and places' (Hallet 2015: 178). Adamski's talk in the *Los Angeles Times*' interview of mind cure and mental science, of applying ancient knowledge to modern life and drawing out the scientific elements it contains fits well with Johnson's theosophical synthesis of Indian wisdom, interplanetary travel, and spirit communication. Hallet also identifies traces in Adamski's writings of Baird Spalding's popular theosophical text, *Life and Teaching of the Masters of the Far East* (1924), not least the borrowing of the title.

In 1940, Adamski and his wife left Laguna Beach, for reasons that remain unclear; several of his relationships with associates and followers ended in breakdown and this may be an early instance. Together with Alice Wells, they set out to form a community on the road to Mount Palomar, first on a small farm and then, in 1944, developing the site around the café at Palomar Gardens. Adamski continued to write. Ray Palmer at *Amazing Stories* claimed he rejected a story in the early 1940s about 'Jesus returning to Earth on board an interplanetary vessel to again spread his message of love and peace' (Hallet 2015: 20), a claim Adamski denied. Adamski certainly produced a text in 1946 called 'The Possibility of Life on Other Planets' which, however, does not speak of the possibility of other life visiting the Earth. And in 1949, he published a science fiction novel, *Pioneers of Space: A Trip to the Moon, Mars and Venus*, described by Hallet as a 'philosophical novel' like the earlier *Satan*.

Hallet suggests *Pioneers* was composed in 1944 (Hallet 2015: 21–22). The amanuensis for the novel was Lucy McGinnis (born 1901), who had worked as a secretary at the Unity School of Christianity in Kansas City,

---

6   *Transmitted Light* is available on the Internet at: babel.hathitrust.org

Missouri, a New Thought organization founded by Myrtle and Charles Fillmore in 1889 (see Satter 1999; Branden 1987). McGinnis had separated from her husband by the time she moved to Palomar Gardens in the early fifties, where she acted as Adamski's secretary; she broke with Adamski in 1961 (Hallet 2015: 23).

In this period, there is evidence both that Adamski developed his interest in sky watching – he was part of the 'Watch the Skies' initiative harnessing civilian volunteers to civil defence and he began taking photographs through a telescope – and that he practised as a spirit medium. It appears it was this combination of interests that drew him together a few years later with Al Bailey and George Williamson.

Spirit communications

Hallet offers a good deal of evidence that Adamski practised as a spirit medium. A young former airman living on the Palomar Gardens property in the Autumn of 1952 saw Adamski in a trance before a group including the Baileys and the Williamsons, revealing he would be contacted shortly by 'a being from another world' (Hallet 2015: 29). This account was confirmed several years later by Williamson to a third party, Williamson speaking of Adamski channelling his 'Tibetan Master' (Hallet 2015: 207).

Adamski would not have been alone in adopting this approach in the period. The first sighting he described, over San Diego on 9 October 1946, had also been witnessed by the medium Mark Probert, who rang Meade Layne, head of the Borderland Sciences Research Associates; Layne 'asked Probert to attempt a telepathic contact with the spacecraft', and called a local radio station to report the attempt. The Los Angeles *Daily News* reported that 'Probert had received a telepathic message from the object, saying that its pilots were from outer space and were seeking contact but were worried about the hostile instinct of mankind'; they wanted 'a meeting with Earth scientists at a remote site' (Hallet 2015: 24).[7]

---

7   Meade Layne was an occultist working in San Diego, who founded the Borderland Sciences Research Associates in February 1945 (Clark 1998: 430). While his

In January 1953, Adamski fell out badly with three men living on the property, one of whom was Williamson, at that point separated from his wife. There are documents relating to this occasion from interviews conducted by the Air Force Office of Special Investigations (OSI) and the FBI, relating to a report (indirectly from Lucy McGinnis, taking Adamski's side in the quarrel) that the men were trying to create 'magnetic frequency machinery similar to the weapons that flying saucers might have', which might be used to shoot down jets in flight (Hallet 2015: 55). The investigation revealed that, in fact, the 'weapons' were Reich-inspired 'orgone cannons' created by one of the visitors, a follower of Wilhelm Reich, and the matter was dropped (Hallet 2015: 56). During the enquiry, Adamski denounced Williamson, claiming the source of the trouble was that 'he [Adamski] was a medium, and that Williamson was not' (Hallet 2015: 55). The three men left the property, but pursued their project; led by Williamson, the men sought to receive extraterrestrial messages and on occasion 'believed themselves "possessed" by entities from other worlds and took extraterrestrial names' (Hallet 2015: 56). Hallet argues this was a technique learnt from Adamski, the more so because two of the names used, Ramu and Firkon, appear in Adamski's second book, *Inside the Spaceships*. Williamson later suggested that the earlier first encounter in the desert might also have been of a psychical nature (Hallet 2015: 39).[8]

Adamski claimed that *Inside the Spaceships* (1955) was based on repeated contacts made between February 1953 and August 1954 (Hallet 2015: 74) (after Williamson and the others had left). The amanuensis in

---

response to the 9 October incident may have offered a model to Adamski (see Clark 1998: 201–202), he also played a wider part in the early framing of flying saucer sightings, which he read in terms of contact with 'etheric' entities living in the Universe in other dimensions – or at other 'densities' – to our own (this is spiritualist language). He understood Arnold's 1947 sighting as 'ether ships' piloted by 'etherians' and made the connection with the science fiction idea of UFOs being visitors from the 'fourth dimension' (Clark 1998: 430); this motif reappears in John Keel's work, with acknowledgement of Layne (see Keele 2014: 156).

8   Williamson continued to search for contact, reappearing in a series of esoteric groups and UFO cults; Hallet gives Moseley and Pflock (2002: 62–63, 136–138, 340–348) as a source.

this instance was a Charlotte Blodget. However, the details of the contacts had already been published in *Pioneers of Space*, written with the assistance of Lucy McGinnis ten years earlier. Adamski pointed to the link when talking to some young men in 1957;[9] he is reported as saying 'I never have had any physical contact with the space brothers, because I already knew all about them and even wrote a book *Pioneers of Space*, describing these things'. He added, 'I learned all that through a unified state of consciousness with what is out there and I never had to have any physical contact with the space brothers' (Hallet 2015: 79). The notion of a 'unified state of consciousness' recurs in Adamski's writing.

Hallet also obtained some letters written by Adamski between August 1950 and May 1952 to a student, Emma Martinelli, living in San Francisco, which give information on how Adamski claimed to have written *Pioneers of Space*. He wrote, 'one may venture from one place to another, while his physical [*sic*] is in one place and he is in another. That is the way I have written this book. I actually have gone to places I speak of …' (Hallet 2015: 80). As Hallet comments, 'this is what occultists call the technique of astral travel'. Adamski linked this business of astral travel to the claim that space people appear on earth to contact chosen subjects, mingling with ordinary people and – except to their contact – unrecognized.

Once we recognize the role of spirit mediumship, we need to re-think the first encounter in the Californian desert in 1952; was it too principally a mental event? In which case, while it is represented by physical elements – flashes in the sky, sightings, photographs, footprints – it does not depend on the consistency of any of these elements to maintain its significance. A focus exclusively on physical elements serves to hide the event, or even to misdirect attention. If this is the case, less attention should be paid to the physical event, and the teaching and example offered by the spaceman seen as central. Yet, all the discussion tends to focus on whether the event occurred or not, to evaluate the evidence in this perspective, and to dismiss the messages as trivial and banal. However, we might assume that the teaching, as esoteric instruction, will not reveal

9   The report appears in the same informant's account that includes the remark by Williamson on Adamski's Tibetan Master (see Hallet's Appendix 3).

its full content readily – it may be impossible to declare it in ordinary language – but will only offer hints in the form of signs and symbols open to being deciphered by those engaged in the secret. The banality of the messages may be a gesture towards inner, hidden truths at the same time as concealing these truths from minds that are not yet ready or, perhaps, unfit to receive them. And last, the major work done by the sighting will be found in the people it draws together, both connecting diverse groups over time and simultaneously making new relationships and breaking established ones. This work will be seen then in the constellations of people formed, in partnerships made and broken, and in the new capacities and perspectives gained by participants or, at least, the promise of these powers and insights, along with enough experience of their realization to make participation in these new social forms worthwhile and, indeed, compelling.

So, when Melton divides alien contacts into two periods – pre- and post-Adamski – the first being made by psychic powers and the second (after Arnold's sighting) by encounter with a UFO (Melton 1995; cf. Jenkins 2013: 48), we can agree with the distinction, but also need to emphasize the continuity between the two forms. UFOs do not simply replace astral travel and, while the content of the messages may shift, as do the scientific discoveries and new technologies being invoked, both the underlying paranormal powers and the motif of instruction in secrets remain remarkably constant. We will return to these issues below.

III. The contact narrative

Adamski's apparently random excursions into the Californian desert seeking contact turned out to be guided by instructions from spirit guides if we follow witnesses' statements (above). He gives hints to the same effect in his account. Adamski was led to the encounter, and his companions may have been chosen to serve as witnesses to the event. We shall look first at the encounter and then the message he received.

The encounter is visually, not to say cinematographically, conceived. Adamski gives a precise time, date and location for the sighting – 12:30 noon on 20 November 1952, '10.2 miles from Desert Center towards Parker, Arizona' (Leslie and Adamski 1953: 189). The group drove into the desert in two cars, past a military base and an airfield, both abandoned, to the base of a mountain ridge. As was his habit, Adamski was guided in his trajectory by 'following … [his] hunches or feelings' (Leslie and Adamski 1953: 191). They left the cars and saw, first, a civilian aircraft over the mountains and then, high up, moving slowly and silently, 'a gigantic cigar-shaped silvery ship, without wings or appendages of any kind' (Leslie and Adamski 1953: 193). This craft drifted towards the observers and then hovered, motionless. Using binoculars, Williamson noticed a marking or insignia on its side. Again following his feelings (or some 'subtler working of the mind' – Leslie and Adamski 1953: 194), Adamski asked to be driven down the road, seeking a place out of sight of the main road. The big ship accompanied them silently, coming to stand high in the air over the car as they went off-road and stopped. Adamski prepared to photograph the spaceship through his telescope.

However, feeling a definite need for haste – a sense which may, in retrospect, have come from 'those in the big ship' (Leslie and Adamski 1953: 195) – he sent the two companions who had driven him back to join the others, half a mile away. As the car left, the ship turned away and disappeared behind the crest of the mountain. At this moment, several Air Force planes went overhead, seeking to engage with the spaceship. The two in the car joined those left behind, and all saw the ship as it 'turned its nose upward and shot out into space, leaving our planes circling' (Leslie and Adamski 1953: 196).

Adamski puts his wish to continue alone, with witnesses at a distance, in perspective; he had had a longstanding desire not only to meet the personnel of some space craft but to take a trip in a saucer, despite the rumours that people so taken up did not return. For this last reason, if taken up, he wanted witnesses to his going. Yet he emphasizes that, although he desired contact, all he had hoped for was a good photograph of a space craft. Nevertheless, 'a beautiful small craft … [drifted into sight] settling silently … about half a mile from me' (Leslie and Adamski 1953: 197), hovering while remaining half-visible to him (because of the terrain) and in full sight of his companions. This allowed Adamski to take a series of pictures, first with his telescopic apparatus and then with a Brownie camera, before the small saucer moved away and disappeared, apparently in response to the return of two of the planes.

We then come to the account of the man from the spaceship. Before we look at this part of the narrative, it is worth extracting certain technical details from their exchanges, details which help explain aspects of the visual sightings. We learn that, just as an aircraft carrier has its naval planes, so the large craft relates to the smaller machine in which the visitor descended to the earth's surface. Moreover, in addition to the 'mother' ship and the 'scout' craft, there were small unmanned disks, remotely controlled, which acted as 'eyes' for the larger spaceship and explained many sightings (Leslie and Adamski 1953: 204–205). We may remark that this tripartite classification had been set out in this form earlier, in Keyhoe (1950b). Adamski also asked about the means of propulsion, receiving the answer that the craft operated by the 'law of magnetic attraction and repulsion'.

At the end of the encounter, the visitor walked with him towards the waiting scout ship, which Adamski describes as a bell-shaped object made of a translucent matter which he took to be treated metal. He speculates that the properties of this material may explain why such craft are elusive to sight and difficult to photograph but nevertheless show up on radar screens (Leslie and Adamski 1953: 212). And these properties, together with the form of propulsion, may explain the variety of coloured lights which have been observed, for the hovering craft reflected rays of light. The top part of the craft was a dome with a ring of glowing coils built into the base, with round portholes in the side wall, through which Adamski glimpsed a second visitor. On top of the craft there was a ball, which Adamski supposed might be part of a propulsion system, drawing the craft through space using the magnetic field, or an attachment device to the mother ship. Beneath the portholes there was a stepped skirt or flange and, beneath that, a three-ball landing gear, half-lowered.

Approaching too close, Adamski ran into a force field, receiving a bruising shock. He gives this as the reason his films, in his jacket pocket, did not come out. The visitor courteously refused his request to enter and look around, and his wish to ride in the spaceship, and then entered the ship by a sliding door. The ship rose silently, displaying two rings under the flange and a third around the centre disk, the two outer circles moving clockwise and the middle one counter-clockwise (Leslie and Adamski 1953: 216). It glided over the crest of the mountains and disappeared into space.

Personal encounter

After the first sighting, when the small space craft had disappeared behind the crest, a man appeared in the same quarter of the landscape and gestured to Adamski, who took him at first for a prospector or a geologist. On approaching the stranger, he saw the man was smaller and younger in appearance than himself, with long hair reaching to his shoulders. As he approached, Adamski's mind became cleared of any sense of caution and he realized he was in the presence of 'A HUMAN BEING FROM ANOTHER WORLD!' (Leslie and Adamski 1953: 199 – caps in original).

He was dressed in a one-piece garment of chocolate brown, with a full blouse and high collar; the sleeves were full, with close-fitting bands at the wrists. An eight-inch band circled his waist, with a golden-brown strip along top and bottom. The trousers resembled the body, being full but held in at the ankles with bands. The garment was made of some fine woven material, without fastenings, pockets or seams. His shoes were made in the same fashion (Leslie and Adamski 1953: 200).

Although the visual description recalls *The Day the Earth Stood Still* and any number of pulp science fiction stories, Adamski presents the meeting in theosophical terms: this is an encounter with an Adept, a Space Master.[10] He describes his initial feelings: the man's beauty of form and his pleasant face 'freed me from all thoughts of my personal self'; Adamski felt 'like a little child in the presence of one of great wisdom and much love, and I became very humble within myself', and the figure radiated 'a

10 We are not, then, dealing with an encounter with an alien life form but with an advanced type of human, a model of what we might become.

feeling of infinite understanding and kindness, with supreme humility' (Leslie and Adamski 1953: 199). The visitor greeted him by extending his arm and touching palms. Adamski comments that in different clothing he could have passed for 'an unusually beautiful woman' (Leslie and Adamski 1953: 199), with a round face, a high forehead, large grey-green eyes, high cheek bones, a chiselled nose, and beautiful teeth. He had no signs of beard growth, and tanned skin, with waving sandy hair, hanging loose. We might notice that spiritual qualities are marked by physical form, including the correlation of higher wisdom with androgyny.

Likewise, their conversation is marked by theosophical motifs. Adamski spoke to the visitor first in words, which were not understood, and then by gesture and telepathy: he formed a picture of a planet in his mind and pointed to the sun, followed by circling motions with his fingers to indicate the orbits of the planets. The man understood, and identified himself as coming from Venus, speaking the word in response to Adamski's articulation in a high-pitched musical tone.

The means having been established, the conversation developed: the Venusians' coming was friendly; they were concerned with radiation from Earth, the result of the explosion of nuclear weapons. The visitor's attitude was compassionate rather than judgmental, as 'toward a much loved child who had erred through ignorance and lack of understanding' (Leslie and Adamski 1953: 203). He indicated not only the effects of radiation were felt out in space, but also it was feared that Earth would be destroyed.

After clarification concerning technical matters (see above), they discussed theology. The visitor affirmed a belief in God as 'Creator of All' but added that 'we on Earth really know very little about this Creator ... Their [understanding] is much broader, and they adhere to the Laws of the Creator instead of laws of materialism as Earth men do ... [In] space ... they live according to the Will of the Creator, not by their own personal will, as we do here on Earth' (Leslie and Adamski 1953: 207).

Adamski then turned the conversation to the question of landings. There have been many visits to Earth from Venus and other planets, including planets in other systems. Space travel was 'a common practice with the people of the other worlds' (Leslie and Adamski 1953: 207). They discussed crashed saucers,[11] and the visitor confirmed that spacemen had died, both through mechanical accidents and human action. And it was explained that landings always took place away from populated areas to prevent human alarm and as precaution against violent reactions against the visitors. However, there would come a time for landings made publicly in populated districts. He also acknowledged that men from Earth had been taken away in space craft.

By now, both parties were reading each other's thoughts as they passed through their minds, although certain matters, such as the varieties of space people and the duration of human evolution, remained unclear. However, they were able to discuss the survival of the mind after death, the visitor pointing to the evolution of human intelligence and indicating that he once lived on Earth but was now, as an advanced being, living in space. Towards the conclusion of the meeting, the visitor broke into another language, construed by Adamski as 'one of the ancient languages spoken here on Earth' (Leslie and Adamski 1953: 211). He made a few deep and distinct footprints, leaving a design to be deciphered; he spoke of matters Adamski was not at liberty to reveal; and he refused to have his photograph taken. They then walked together to the scout craft.

The combination of great wisdom and extraordinary mental powers, the sense of compassion for the human condition matched by the need on the human side for education, the cosmic setting and interplanetary commerce, the placing of human ignorance and the advanced understanding of the spacemen in an evolutionary perspective organized by repeated incarnation, all signal a theosophical understanding within which contemporary signs and wonders – sightings and landings – can be interpreted. The Space Brothers are Adepts, without addition or subtraction.

---

11 For details on the contemporary interest in 'crashes and retrievals of UFOs', see Clark (1998: 119–141). I have mentioned the early influence of Skully (1950) above.

Publication

The publication of Adamski's account gives indications of the wider intellectual and social context and his setting within a specific milieu. In the first place, his account was ghost-written by Clara L. John (Clark 1998: 20), who was part of a wider network. By the mid-50s John edited a contactee-oriented newsletter and organized a monthly Flying Saucer Discussion Group in Washington DC, out of which the National Investigations Committee on Aerial Phenomena (NICAP) emerged in 1956 (see Clark 1998: 411–414).[12]

In the second place, his account was appended by John to an already-completed manuscript by a British writer, Desmond Leslie. This was logical, given Adamski's approach, for Leslie's work sets flying saucer sightings in the context of theosophical evolutionary history and physics, citing Blavatsky, Besant, Leadbeater, A. E. Powell, Alice Bailey and Scott Elliot. This is how he begins:

> About eighteen million years ago ... at a time when Mars, Venus and Earth were in close conjunction, along a magnetic path so formed came a huge, shining, radiant vessel of dazzling power and beauty, bringing to earth 'thrice thirty-five' human beings, of perfection beyond our highest ideals; gods rather than men; divine kings of archaic memory, under whose benign world-government a shambling, hermaphrodite monster was evolving into thinking, sexual man'. (Leslie and Adamski 1953: 6)

He then turns to speculations arising from theosophical physics about the transformation of energy and new means of propulsion revealed by the spaceships, together with the interest modern governments show in the novel form of locomotion, an interest which, however, they conceal from public gaze. These three themes – human evolution in a theosophical perspective, an alternative physics, and the history of sightings (extended backwards in time by use of Charles Fort's writings) – structure

---

12 Peebles suggests that John developed Adamski's original manuscript and that both Bailey and Williamson denied the published version of events; he cites Moseley's (1955) investigation (Peebles 1994: 97–98; James Moseley, in 'Special Adamski Exposé Issue', *Saucer News*, October 1957).

the book and allow the introduction of Adamski as the latest episode, with a seasoning of paranoia concerning secret state and commercial interests in obscuring the true import of these sightings from the public.

We may understand that Adamski and his group of companions were by no means isolated, even if they were marginal figures within the wider milieu, and this may be confirmed by the successful sales figure for the book. To some extent, it is the contradictions of the milieu that are played out in the history of conflicts and separations that mark Adamski's later history; it also reflects the fissile nature of groups organized around imponderable secrets.

IV. Inside the Spaceships

Adamski quickly published a second book, *Inside the Spaceships* (1955), which developed the themes introduced in the earlier essay. It is constructed around a series of identical episodes, with minor variations, which run as follows. Adamski is first contacted mentally by the spacemen so that he goes to a hotel in Los Angeles, where he is met by two men who are in fact spacemen, working incognito on an information-gathering mission, who drive him out of town to a waiting scout craft. The pilot carries Adamski and his companions to a mother ship, where he is feted and shown various technological wonders, including a magnetic propulsion system, graphic displays, and devices for the remote monitoring of the earth's inhabitants; he is also given glimpses of settlements on the Moon and the hosts' planets through a viewing device and 3-D projections. However, the focus on each occasion is that he is addressed by a Space Master, who delivers a discourse which is then elucidated, after the Master has left, by discussion with his companions. Finally, he is returned to his hotel to consider what he has heard. The crucial chapters do not, then, primarily concern explanations of space flight technology, nor the listening and communication devices, nor the glimpses of life on other planets; rather, these elements are integrated into the discourses he hears and records (retained in his memory with telepathic help) from the Masters who have sent for him and who acknowledge his worth.

The teaching he receives is constructed around a conventional theosophical account of the cosmological order and of the place of humans in an evolutionary scheme, and it centres on the topics of Universal Brotherhood and Loving Service, in both cases echoing themes from Adamski's Laguna Beach days. The book is concerned to present Adamski's teaching and to confirm his vocation; while he describes himself as a disciple, his Masters' teachings are in fact his own, and his status as an Adept is affirmed for any enlightened reader to see.

First discourse

The first discourse (found in Adamski 1953, chapter 5) is given telepathically by a 'greatly evolved being', who begins from a cosmological perspective: space is 'constantly active, filled with moving particles from out of which all forms are finally brought into being. There is neither a beginning nor an ending'.[13] This progressive rule of growth applies to the innumerable planets, which he speaks of in terms of their ability to support the human form: the planets are 'mostly peopled and governed by forms like yourselves'; some are reaching a point of being able to support such forms, others have not yet reached this stage of development, yet others are intellectually and socially advanced compared with Earth. Progress is linked to adhering to the laws of Nature, that is, 'following the laws of the All Supreme Intelligence which governs all time and space'. And the ability to travel between planets – 'the traversing of space' – is evidence of having 'mastered the laws within which all bodies live and move – planets and men alike'. All beings share this desire to progress. 'The inhabitants of other worlds are not [then] fundamentally different from Earth men … The purpose of life on other worlds is basically the same as yours … the yearning to rise to something higher'. For man progresses – in life,

---

13 I have not given pages numbers for citations because I used an on-line text of *Inside the Spaceships* which lacked them.

from planet to planet, from system to system – 'towards an ever-higher understanding and evolvement in universal growth and service'. This account introduces the two themes of universal brotherhood and loving service: men from all planets are part of the same scheme and their task is to assist each other to progress.

Here, however, a critical note is heard. For men on Earth do not fully understand either theme, being only at an intermediate level of advancement. The Master uses the example of the principles of space travel by the control of gravity, allowing the overcoming of distance and time, adding 'we would gladly give you this knowledge ... except that you have not yet learned to live with one another in peace and brotherhood, for the welfare of all men alike'. Indeed, the spacemen fear the possibility of Earth's aggression towards space, starting with the desire to use the Moon as a military base. As men reform, more will be revealed to them. Adamski's task is then to warn of the dangers facing the Earth, and to point to the possibility of progress. All Earth lacks is an understanding of 'the One Supreme Being', and he repeats the motif of the earlier first encounter: Spacemen live by the Creator's laws, while on Earth, we only talk about them. This is a personal vocation and a unique call: people are weary of strife, suspicion and censure; they 'hunger for knowledge of a way of life that will deliver them'. Adamski can give them this knowledge, that progress in scientific knowledge needs to be accompanied by increasing moral and spiritual understanding.

These themes are reiterated and developed in conversations between Adamski and his companions once the Master has left them (Adamski 1953, chapter 6).[14] Spacemen, more advanced than Earthmen, know that every individual, every intelligent life form, must 'decide its own destiny without interference from another'; this principle is in conformity with the universal laws, which have objective reality. The spacemen's only option is to offer counsel and teaching by telepathic and other means: they emit mental warnings to awaken Earth people to the disasters they are bringing on themselves, offer evidence in support of these thoughts in the form of

14 The Masters who address Adamski are of a higher order than his initial contacts. We might also notice that, despite his initial awe, Adamski has become a companion and equal to these intermediaries.

flying saucer sightings, and make secret high-level contacts with Earth governments officials. They cannot intervene more directly. This combination of principles and limitations explain the grounds for Adamski's selection and training and define his mission; he has shown both the necessary receptivity and commitment for the role of mediator.

We also learn something about the telepathic communication between Adamski and his mentors: telepathy is compared to sending messages over radio waves, yet without any instrument – from brain to brain, over any distance. These contacts are distinguished from 'psychic' or 'spiritualistic' messages. The mentors can both receive his thoughts and send him information 'exactly as … a message over a telephone … we call this mental telepathy a *unified state of consciousness* between two points, the sender and the receiver, and it is the method of communication most commonly used on our planets'.

Second discourse

Taken on a visit to a second spaceship, Adamski met another Master (Adamski 1953, chapter 10), an equally remarkable figure who, he felt, 'was no stranger to me, and for whom I felt instantly the deepest affection and a kind of kinship … His presence added immeasurably to the feeling of harmony and understanding among all of us gathered in the room'. He sensed that the Master was 'capable of looking at my every thought' and that he understood his human protégé without judging him; his glance was 'full of a great kindness' and his face was 'endlessly refined by the Spirit that dwells therein'. We might note the stilted language Adamski used. We are later told this Master is 'one of the most evolved beings still functioning within our system'.

In the previous chapter, Adamski had been shown instruments used to analyse the Earth's atmosphere and had seen for himself the behaviour of 'the … force that pervades all space, from which planets, suns and galaxies are formed; the same force that is the supporter and sustainer of all activity and life throughout the Universe'. This force is displayed through the equipment as 'whirling energy, solidification, disintegration; a perpetual motion of energy and fine matter ever seeking to combine or react with other particles in space'. The Master began his discourse from this insight into cosmic energies and the unifying principle behind all matter. There is a unity to all forms, from dust particles to planets and suns without number; 'all are bathed in the sea of One Power, supported by the One Life'. All forms have a degree of intelligence, expressing the thought of the Intelligence of the Divine Creator. If we focus this understanding in human terms, all are brothers and sisters. Moreover, in this perspective the rule of life is progress, and all states will be experienced. Since the body is a temporary dwelling, matters such as colour and nationality are incidental, and the names of forms are irrelevant, for all forms dwell in 'the Complete'.[15]

An ethic of service follows directly from this cosmological principle of brotherhood: 'Each form expresses its purpose and renders the service for which it was made ... [B]y serving willingly, [all forms] grow in understanding of the source from which they receive their wisdom'. In this fashion, each life form contributes to the whole by service.

Once again, the Master changed direction at this point to offer a diagnosis of Earth people's shortcomings, for men on Earth understand neither the condition of Universal Brotherhood – the Unity of Creation – nor the accompanying ethic of service. Instead, men lack understanding, they usurp the capacity for judgement and so destroy harmony. Each man lives in enmity with his neighbours; although all desire peace, each lives in confusion, in dread and in fear of death. There is a considerable passage on man's living in ignorance and fear and his being bound up in material concerns and neglecting the eternal.

The Master concluded by encouraging Adamski, strengthening him to face ridicule and disbelief, and promising him both that more people will

---

15   This last claim is significant on two counts. First, the spacemen use names in a fashion unlike our own which is not explained, so the names Adamski attributes to the visitors – Orthon (the name of his first contact), Ramu, Firkon et alia – are simply for identification in the narrative. Second, when details of the visits to the planets were challenged on the ground of increasing knowledge of conditions on Saturn, Venus and the Moon, it could be claimed that these names too were symbolic and referred to more distant systems than our own.

hear his message and that he always will be able mentally to contact the spacemen. Adamski returned to Earth a new man, resolved to serve 'the One Intelligence as man is intended to, and for which purpose he was created'.

Third discourse

The third and last discourse was also delivered by the second Master (Adamski 1953, chapter 12). He returned to the same topics, this time extending the analysis of human limitations and focussing on human potential in terms both of powers and calling. While space people realize 'the relationship and interdependence of all things', Earth people have a custom of dividing things; the analysis builds on this distinction. Space people know that all forms have the Deity within them, through which everything takes part in the law of Evolution or Transmutation; they understand that all life comes from Him. Minerals and elements are combined according to instruction, and in fulfilling its potential, each mineral rises to another level and progresses. As an instance, iron can 'rise' to carry an electric charge and fulfil a 'better' service, becoming magnetic and gaining the power of attraction. In like fashion, man may follow the divine path by ordering matter, fulfilling his purpose, and thereby rising to new powers and possibilities.

This argument allows the Master to refine an account of human experience and sensitivity. Earth men have divided what needs be considered as one, and in so doing have lost any sense of divine purpose. With respect to experience, we have lost sight of our true identity and divided the senses arbitrarily into five, needing then to add further capacities beyond the normal senses, again arbitrarily split into 'powers of clairvoyance, clairaudience, mental telepathy, or extra-sensory perception'. And we are given brief instruction in how the unity of the physical senses is to be found in the primacy of touch, for touch is a feeling and so a manifestation of the all-inclusive intelligence and gives form to the other physical sensations of sight, hearing, taste and smell.

Repeating the motif discerned in mineral life, the elements in the body serve the intelligence, for good or ill. Understanding the presence of this underlying ordering reason allows a man to free himself, escaping his limited prison and becoming a dweller of the Universe. For he sees the law in operation, he knows himself and (through knowing himself) knows all things, and comes in this way to know his Creator, the Universal, Divine Intelligence. In this fashion, material man may rise to a state of unity with the Father. Earth men, the Master says, are like the Prodigal Son; they are (we might say) lost among the minerals; they must come to their senses and return to the Father. The basic questions, then, the Master tells Adamski, and the key to his teaching, are these: 'Who am I? Through what avenues can I express in order to return to the oneness from which I have fallen?'

Once man learns who he is and begins to live this understanding, his woes will vanish and his four senses (*sic*) will evolve, serving in both the physical world and the universal, for everything takes place within the Supreme Intelligence. Understanding the unity of everything both alters the enlightened person's powers of sensitivity and perception and adjusts his ethical commitment to the whole. More, the universal perspective explains why men from other planets are concerned with this world, and Adamski with the fate of his fellows, for the higher forms are called to help the lower to realize themselves. This is the ethic of loving service.

The Master concludes with the topics of death and eating other forms of life, both of which are framed in terms of transmutation in a perspective of progress. As we live in a constant present, as forms of the Divine Intelligence realized as minds housed in a variety of bodies, death is swallowed up in a sequence of rebirths, which is likened to travel between planets. The issue then is to choose to be master of the material condition, instead of being mastered by it. In the end, this comes down to a matter of capacity and will and defines both Adamski's vocation and task: he is to instruct the people of Earth – or those capable of receiving the message – in this crucial insight.

Universal brotherhood and the ethic of loving service form the core of the Masters' teaching, and we have learnt something of their advanced mental powers and the accompanying cosmology. We might notice in passing that, from the human perspective, willpower stands as our only means of connecting the individual with the Universal; intermediate scale phenomena such as social relations serve only as an index of the moral state achieved. Yet a variety of other, potentially sociological topics emerge in the discussions with space brothers (and sisters)[16] in the margins of these central episodes. We get glimpses of the work of operatives on mission on Earth and, similarly, some information about life on the home planets. We gain a sense of their advanced ethics and pacific way of life, founded around love and non-possessiveness, as well as their practices of collective ritual dance (in contrast to individualistic American dancing) as part of both education and religion. We also have some insight into their advanced technologies, harnessing magnetism, optics and static electricity for the purposes of travel and observation; there are devices for recording and monitoring thought-vibrations, allowing the translation of languages, reading minds, and creating exhaustive historical records. We gain a sense of the long-term history of the Earth, of human origins, of our troubled common life, and of the intervention of people from other planets in the form of prophets and other religious leaders who have attempted to ameliorate these troubles. We have discussion of various UFO incidents and their possible significance in this perspective. We also learn about the role human spiritual blindness plays in creating ageing and disease, and our potential through awareness of putting these problems behind us, as well as of gaining access to memories of past lives in our future forms.

In short, Adamski's message is that we have it within our power to make things better, indeed, that our everyday life could be realized perfectly, without the fears and traumas inflicted by biology and our social arrangements. This is a transposition of spiritualist belief, summed up in the picture of Divinity displayed on the walls of the spaceship, 'the radiant portrait of Ageless Life', inflected through the theosophical lens.

---

16 Although Adamski remarked on the androgynous beauty of the space brothers in the first encounter, he equally notes the feminine beauty of the women in the spaceships, together with their flowing dresses and jewellery when relaxing and their tight-fitting uniforms when working as pilots. There is material here to be developed.

V. Disputes

The discourses recorded in *Inside the Spaceships* display Adamski's theosophical understanding, which he could clothe without distortion in materials taken from contemporary technological and security projects. Not much effort of adaptation was required. His central concerns were with establishing his credentials and offering a means of healing to the surrounding society, repair in the form of a progressive initiation into an integrated understanding of the world and the human place in it, given substance by gathering a group of elect followers who were promised both the possibility of gaining advanced mental powers and of playing a role in the restoration of a fully human social order. Even the technologies described were focussed around theosophical ideas, being concerned with making many kinds of information immediately present to the elect by overcoming problems of scale, distance, time and communication.

Through this approach, Adamski was able to make several connections. Most importantly, he prolonged his earlier life and role in Laguna Beach, with one set of colleagues, into his work on Mount Palomar, with another. There, he succeeded in gathering a loose community around himself, acting as a part of a wider network through which people passed, those in transit often separating from former friends, spouses and workmates and forming new associations of a temporary or more enduring nature. Not only the liaisons and separations, but also Adamski's financing, his visitors, secretarial aid, the newsletters supporting the network, his writing and publishing were all made possible by the authority and energies created by the contacts with flying saucers.[17] The 'incidents' (sightings, contacts), then, despite the careful and contested witness borne to their positive occurrence by photographs, testimonies and other evidence, were significant rather because of the people they separated and brought together in different ways, not

17 In this regard it is worth noting the repeated comments by associates on Adamski's brief connections with space brothers in hotels in both Los Angeles and on his European tours (e.g. Zinsstag and Good 1983: 30 f.); these too were permitted by the social energies at work.

because of any specific content; distinct times and constellations of people were connected by these relays which were largely without defined content.

There are severe limits to any group constituted in this informal fashion around what we may call a secret, an imponderable truth to which members subscribe (cf. Jenkins 1999, 2013). The group is formed by each member advancing in the secret around which it is organized, and it is held together by the promise of gaining access to higher levels of esoteric knowledge, and it recruits by contagion, for outsiders become apprised of the secret and wish to know more. A member will then join for one reason and gain other motives as he or she reaches higher levels of understanding, and there is often a tension between ethical motives for joining and the more instrumental aims of higher learning. But the main challenge to the group is the other face of its spreading by contagion: it is always threatened by betrayal of the secret, by disappointed participants who have attained only limited insight allowing uninitiated outsiders to make ill-informed judgements, and by splits emerging once the authority of the leaders is questioned. Because of their lack of organization, these groups are inherently fissile.

Adamski's loosely ordered group had a characteristic history in this regard. In the mid-1950s, Lucy McGinnis edited a newsletter which allowed Adamski to keep in touch with a range of people who had gained an interest in his role as an intermediary with the space people, and readers also had an active role, exchanging letters with one another. This was not necessarily distinguishable from the science fiction 'fanzine' culture which began in the 1930s (see Keel 2014: 117f.) and which was flourishing by the 1950s. Lou Zinsstag, a cousin of C. G. Jung living in Zurich, contacted Adamski in 1954 and joined this 'letter circle' of correspondents; she organized two European visits for Adamski in 1959 and 1963, and has given an account of her association with him (Zinsstag and Good 1983). Her account is of interest because of her insider status and for the narrative she gives of internal division and external opposition, the last framed in an idiosyncratic way. The ostensible reason for a series of defections was Adamski's equivocation around whether he had observed the visitors and their machines in the fashion he described, as a positive experience, or whether he had made contact as a spirit medium and channelled his reports. His followers believed the former to be the case until doubt set in. This was reported to be

McGinnis's reason for breaking with Adamski in 1961 (Zinsstag and Good 1983: 85), and her leaving formed the point at which, in Zinsstag's view, matters began to go wrong. There is evidence that Adamski had denounced spiritualist activities – for example, in a 1959 newsletter, he announced himself in favour of telepathy but against trance messages (Zinsstag and Good 1983: 55) – but, as we have seen, his commitment to spirit contacts went back much further than 1961. Madame Blavatsky, of course, tried to make the same distinction: she received messages from Adepts who were actual men even if they shared many of the properties of spirits.

McGinnis was replaced by Carol Honey, a man working as a technician for Hughes Aircraft, who took over the newsletter, producing the first *Cosmic Science newsletter* in January 1962. In the March issue, Adamski spoke of a prospective space visit, from which he would return with both general and secret information, the latter meant privately for world leaders. He asked his co-workers to tune into his thoughts from Saturn, giving times and dates. In June, he reported in the newsletter on his trip to Saturn, and published pamphlets, *Saturn Trip I & II*, in which he claimed to have experienced a new form of propulsion, travelling at the speed of thought to attend a meeting of an Interplanetary Council (see Hallet 2015: 129ff.). His followers noted possible contradictions between the two published versions.

Adamski had already displayed sensitivity to possible opposition in the March newsletter, expressing a desire to investigate his companions and perhaps check on their loyalty, saying that, as well as receiving the information referred to, he would also 'review the past lives of those who are working with me and why they are associated with me at this time' (Zinsstag and Good 1983: 67). Zinsstag describes this visit to Saturn as 'a personal mental experience of Adamski, induced by some method of self-hypnosis' (Zinsstag and Good 1983: 70). In partial confirmation, Adamski wrote in the September newsletter that riding in spaceships demands 'blend[ing] their [the travellers'] consciousness with All-Consciousness ... [also called] Cosmic Consciousness' (Zinsstag and Good 1983: 77). Zinsstag, however, attributes this alteration to his being manipulated by enemies, either by his being contacted by a 'new set of [space] boys' (Zinsstag and Good 1983: 60, 71), who, unlike the first visitors, were unfavourable to human contacts and fed him wrong information, or by having his mind controlled at a distance by secret agents.[18] The view that Adamski was being ill-advised and manipulated by his contacts became widely shared among his co-workers.

Adamski's relationship with Honey, who had originally been appointed as his 'representative in the United States' (Hallet 2015: 126–127), also deteriorated. In September 1962, Adamski announced he had been given a new assignment, to work 'in close contact with Cosmic Principle' (Zinsstag and Good 1983: 76), and he asked Honey to take over the 'Get Acquainted Program'[19] while he concentrated on cosmic philosophy and cosmic science, basic ethical issues and Christ's teachings (Zinsstag and Good 1983: 77). Like Adamski, Honey published a practical booklet on telepathy;[20] he rejected 'psychic or astral contacts with space people', and distinguished telepathy from trance (Zinsstag and Good 1983: 79). By 1963, the two had fallen out, and the co-workers divided into two camps. The issue was around travel while in a mediumistic state. Honey stated in a letter he was present when 'Mr A. went into a trance and claimed Orthon was talking through his vocal cords' (Zinsstag and Good 1983: 81). Honey, however, defended Adamski's first contacts as authentic and portrayed him as being subsequently deceived, even hypnotized, by his space brothers (Zinsstag and Good 1983: 83). Honey announced a purge among the space people, with the aim of eliminating the influence of the recent space brothers (Zinsstag and Good 1983: 82). He continued to publish a newsletter with an increasingly religious focus (paralleling Adamski's path). Some of Adamski's supporters among the co-workers suspected Honey was a state-sponsored agent of disruption within the group, citing the fact that, at the time, he

---

18   She cites Keel's *Operation Trojan Horse* (1970) and Walter Bowart's *Operation Mind Control* (1978).
19   The purpose of the program was to identify spacemen working incognito on Earth, initially making a rendezvous by telepathy, and then catching the eye of an apparent stranger in a public place – exchanging a look – to establish sympathetic contact. Zinsstag and Good both give instances of such close encounters; speech was not exchanged on either occasion. Adamski had psychic qualities the others lacked which allowed him to establish communication with these space brothers.
20   Adamski had produced an account of *Telepathy – The Cosmic or Universal Language* in 1958.

was working on part of the space programme. Zinsstag's view was that both Adamski and Honey may have been manipulated by 'some impersonators in their own groups' (Zinsstag and Good 1983: 86), that is, by spacemen passing for humans infiltrated among the co-workers. Paranoid discriminations therefore become finer and finer: it is increasingly hard to tell who is a spaceman and who a human, who is acting deceptively and who has been manipulated or deceived. Friends and enemies become intimately confused. Adamski saw the rift in his co-workers in terms of propaganda and the work of a 'vicious group' deceiving Honey (Zinsstag and Good 1983: 80–81). Towards the end of his career, he was sure a 'Silence Group' was active in obstructing his work, although he was never clear as to the source of interference; he mentioned the CIA, government scientists, even some space brothers and their contacts (Hallet 2015: 147–148).[21] In his last book, *Flying Saucers Farewell* (1961) (produced with Honey's assistance), Adamski expressed the view that the Silence Group was active in disrupting his European tour in 1959, particularly in Zurich, where financial interests are concentrated, and introduced an anti-Semitic note (Hallet 2015: 120). The Silence Group also appears in the *Saturn Trip* pamphlets, where similarities in the criticism of two former collaborators is cited as evidence of conspiracy (Hallet 2015: 130). But these ideas had been present in his work from the beginning, in the notion that commercial energy interests were concerned to discredit talk of flying saucers because of the revolutionary potential of their propulsion technology.

If we follow Zinsstag, Adamski's co-workers used these ideas to construct a history: space people initially made contact in the aftermath of the War, sensing a human openness and need for help; Adamski was a key part of this opportunity, through whom they passed 'a description of their code of living and some simple advice' (Zinsstag and Good 1983: 92). However, their policy changed in light of human responses; the visitors were put off by the breakdown of Air Force and Government attitudes in 1952,

---

21 The idea of a Silence Group was probably taken over from Gray Barker, who invented the phrase 'Men in Black' in 1954, drawing on the experiences of Dahl and Crisman, Albert Bender, and the Robertson panel report – see Clark (1998: 376–386). Keyhoe (1953) (as we have seen) developed a similar account.

presumably after the Washington incident (Zinsstag and Good 1983: 93). Paralleling human shifts in policy, we can detect a change in spacemen's behaviour; Adamski too, in this account, became a disappointment to his space patrons, betraying their cause by turning to hypnosis and trance. By the late 1960s it had become a widely held view that spacemen were deceivers (see Keel 1970; Vallee 1969) and interchangeable with government agents; Adamski's circle were early in perceiving these possibilities. As suggested above, unexpected outcomes, disappointments and the like can always be attributed to a shift in power within one or another hidden group. Good, paraphrasing a newsletter from Adamski to his co-workers in July 1963, sums the problem up: 'Spacemen are masters in the art of camouflage and subterfuge, employing sophisticated methods of hypnotism, thought-transference, projected images, and other forms of mental manipulation' (Zinsstag and Good 1983: 196); moreover, they are not all well-intentioned.

Adamski continued to write, producing *Cosmic Philosophy* in 1961 (the most comprehensive introduction to his thought, in Good's view), and *The Science of Life Study Course* in 1964 (both published by the George Adamski Foundation). The last recycled text from the 1936 *Wisdom of the Masters of the Far East*, with 'space brothers' substituted for 'The Royal Order of Tibet'. In the context of the quarrels, this fact was seized upon as evidence of fraudulence, but it is possible to view Adamski's life as dedicated to a single project of education and enlightenment, and to suppose that he recycled materials in part because of limited literacy.[22] He had a continuing ambition to form a community around the teachings he had received (he was hoping to form another such a community in Mexico – Hallet 2015: 149) and was producing materials to train a new generation of leaders. He died in 1965. Alice Wells' obituary published a year later portrayed him as a Teacher of the Science of Life, teaching obedience to Nature's Cosmic Laws and sharing Understanding of Cosmic Intelligence. In an earlier account, published for readers of the *Cosmic Bulletin* in June 1965, a more intimate circle, she claimed that, in common with other men of high Cosmic Consciousness

---

22 We may also note in this regard that the text of *Satan, Man of the Hour* (1937) is used again in *Flying Saucers Farewell* (1961) – see Hallet (2015: 19).

Awareness, he was a member of the Interplanetary Council (as had been revealed in *Saturn Trip*), and that he was being granted a new body so that his intelligence could pursue his cosmic mission (Hallet 2015: 170). These two tributes nicely sum up the position for Adamski's followers: while the outside world might know him as a teacher and enquirer after truth, the insider knew him to be an Adept, a member of a higher race with a mission and powers we can only guess at.

Groups parallel and derivative

It is worth remarking, before discussing some of the patterns that emerge in Adamski's life, that his social circle was by no means unique in the period; we have both independent instances of the same kind and ones that owned a kinship with his, each a version of the theodicy created by the theosophists in the 1880s incorporating ideas drawn from evolutionary theory and from the physical sciences and living out their implications.

Following Adamski's initiative, a range of contactees emerged. Starting from the perspective of the ufologist, Clark points to the readiness with which mediums followed Adamski's lead (Clark 1998: 104–114) and identifies Dorothy Martin as among the first psychic contacts; she is the Mrs Keech of Festinger's classic study (Festinger et al. 1956).[23] Mrs Keech adopted many elements of the same world-view: spirit contacts from a race of spacemen engaged in interplanetary travel who, in previous incarnations, had visited Earth; the cosmic vocation to monitor the Earth and its troubles; their use of advanced mental powers to test and train recruits as

23 Adamski's career in some respects resembles that of a typical medium, sketched by Moore (1977: 125–126), who suggests a pattern of a solitary early life followed by a period of impressing adults, a later gilding of trickery because of the demands of performance and the pressure of competition, followed by a retrospective sense of self-doubt or, at least, opposition and persecution. This pattern also appears in the context of Madame Blavatsky's work and life. Moore's account misses out the element of apprenticeship and, more generally, the collective features enabling such a life, including the role of the media, but it fits quite well.

part of this mission; the annunciation of an approaching catastrophe that threated all human life; the promise to transport a selected few to another planet to train and then return them to help recover human civilization; the presence on Earth of spacemen who could only be recognized by those in the know; the play of esoteric and common knowledge; and the stiffening of human opposition to those contacted as a sign of the coming crisis and its planned resolution. All these motifs match up with Adamski's teaching and indicate resources being shared by a wider milieu.[24]

An example of a parallel but independent group with many of the same sociological characteristics, though with a somewhat different take on the Blavatskyan inheritance, is given in Pendle's biography of the rocket engineer Jack Parsons (Pendle 2005). Parsons was one of the founders of the Jet Propulsion Laboratory at Caltech and a pioneer in the development of rocket propulsion who died in an explosion in June 1952 in Pasadena, a city northeast of Los Angeles. Like Adamski, he was an autodidact with limited formal education, a consumer of science fiction pulps, a poet and informal teacher, with a long history of involvement in occult groups. He lived in a community called the Church of Thelema, which pursued the teachings of Aleister Crowley. Crowley was a product of the darker side of Theosophy who had reshaped an order called the Ordo Templis Orientis (O.T.O.) (see Owen 2004: 217–218), which set up a branch in California in the 1930s. Parsons joined the 'Agape Lodge' in 1941, where he became a leading member of the group. It differed in many respects from Adamski's community, for the lodge was a secret society with closed membership, dedicated to experiments with art, sex and drugs, exploring their possibilities as means of gaining direct contact with the Cosmic Mind. But there were similarities. The O.T.O. lived out the non-possessive ethic of love glimpsed by Adamski in his visit to Saturn, and the magic practised was another working-out of theosophical ideas we have met with as astral travel, organized around levels of initiation; the purpose of the magic was to allow the mind to transcend the limitations of the material world and

---

24 For a survey of the wider milieu, including more recent groups awaiting the arrival of flying saucers, see Lewis (1995) and Partridge (2003).

its illusions, and to gain power through freeing mental experience to join with a higher reality.

Parsons' decline was assisted by L. Ron Hubbard, who relieved him both of a mistress and his money through an investment he persuaded him to make; Hubbard later claimed to have been investigating him on behalf of Naval Intelligence. Parsons' last days were spent under investigation by the FBI for transferring rocket secrets to Israel while he was working for Hughes Aircraft Co.; after his death Parsons, who did not keep his explosives work and his magic fully separate, was replaced by German rocket scientists. Hubbard, of course, succeeded where Crowley and Parsons (and indeed Adamski) failed: he created a successful and lasting religious institution – Scientology – around a theory of mind, the therapeutic practice of Dianetics, which was first published in *Astounding Science Fiction* in 1950 (Urban 2011).

Both groups confirm features identified in Adamski's lifework. They represent alliances with machinery (or the spirit of advanced technology) to achieve specific ends. If we leave Parsons to one side for, despite many similarities, his focus on magic was necessarily a private preoccupation, both Keech and Adamski allowed members of the public to join them and to seek instruction in secrets to heal both themselves and the wider society: they presented an apologetic message focussed around the acceptance of the existence of space people. Accepting the existence of spacemen involved taking on both a series of cosmological claims – the linking of physical and mental powers, the implication of souls and bodies, a continuous scale of matter and being – and a series of political diagnoses concerning American culture and the prospects for peace. If you accepted the messengers at their own evaluation and made the message your own, you rejected corruption, you were cured of your incompleteness, and you shared in the healing of the fragmented state of the world. And, despite the surface differences concerning the techniques employed to contact the powers in question, that was also the programme of the O.T.O.

A feature worth remarking in all three cases is the absence of children: while these groups were concerned with moral visions of the human future, they had no practical stake in that future. There is then a noteworthy sterility to these realizations of the New Age, these prototypes of the Coming Race. It is a question whether this feature corresponds to a sacrifice made to the common good and perhaps a correlate to the notion of Universal Brotherhood; it may also have to do with the notion of the reincarnation of the monad in successive bodies, so that the progress of the individual spirit trumps any ideas of kinship and descent, while alliances are considered contingent and instrumental.

VI. Sociological implications

What of more general significance comes out of this account of Adamski's life? We might begin by observing that Adamski, because of his commitment to theosophical teaching, articulates the real source of the interplanetary hypothesis, whatever its subsequent scientific justification. The rejection of his account by both advocates and opponents of the hypothesis could then be taken as indicating a sociological question of some interest. How can we characterize the sociological implications of the link we have traced between Theosophy and the social dynamics of the group within which theosophical ideas are expressed? The two are joined around the defence and detection of secrets, and this project can be described first in formal terms as a distinctive structure of thought which eliminates any consideration of social analysis, and second in positive terms as a rhetorical approach aimed at persuasion. It has two faces, then, combining an apologetic approach (in a technical, religious sense), aimed at recruiting members and relating to outsiders, with a non-social self-imagining. This combination, we will find, may be related to a specific understanding or model of language, distinct from that identified in Keyhoe and Menzel, and to certain organizational features. A sociological description of this kind, drawing on the documents available in this case, can tell us a good deal of more general application about the networks of individuals and groups concerned with flying saucers, both for and against.

Reduction

To sum up features of the previous description, Adamski presents his story by focussing on certain elements and ignoring or pushing others to the background. Notably, he highlights the relation between the visitors from space and military and technological organizations in America which both represent authoritative knowledge and exhibit a tendency to withhold information, in short, which hold secret knowledge. This relationship is presented in a manner that draws on films of the period, with a presentation of visualized scenes relying on a series of flashbacks to disclose and re-frame information. This world is realistic, in that it can be recorded on film, but time cannot be trusted: it must be re-ordered to make sense; editing – or, more accurately, re-editing – is a condition of truth-telling. In these representations, flying saucers are conceived within a technological and security frame: they are machines, borrowing elements from contemporary developments in missile flight, experimental aircraft, radar, new materials, communications systems and so forth. But a good deal is left out of this picture. The contribution of science fiction is not mentioned, the work of the press is minimized, and the complex history of theosophical projects, intentional communities and networks of publication and dissemination of ideas is ignored. We are offered a radical simplification, clearing the ground with the aim of presenting a narrative centred around ideas of conspiracy and deciphering a secret. Indeed, the narrative of conspiracy and its gradual deciphering trumps all other concerns, such as scientific ideas, technical solutions, military and international threats, let alone considerations of any personal kind; all are put to work as elements in a story controlled by the notion of secrets operating at a large scale. As an example, we might note that the motif of the potential contained in the flying saucers' technologies of space flight and propulsion is only a device to allow the introduction of a mysterious 'silence group', who seek to discredit the notion of visitors from space with the sole end of defending commercial interests invested in current energy production from competition. This kind of thinking operates neither at the level of state interests nor at that of the family and its dramas: it is another kind of activity, concerned with getting things done by forging alliances with these new machines to achieve a series of ends, both personal and cosmic, against the grain.

For, at the same time, the intermediate scale of events and relationships occluded by this selection and presentation of details continues to operate and make itself felt. The observation of flying saucers allows the creation, over time, of all sorts of new relationships, establishing contacts, forming constellations and networks, linking different periods and groups, and allowing new capacities to emerge in individuals; in short, it creates the potential to shift roles and, in this way, to contribute in new guises to state and personal enterprises. The other side of these new relationships is a series of exclusions, breaking contacts, forgetting people and abandoning projects, refocussing energies, and letting other capacities wane. These changes are in practice most readily monitored in terms of the splits that occur, which in this instance often arise around the presenting issue of whether flying saucers are physically present ('on film') or not. Yet as we have seen, these two positions are not symmetrical or equivalent, for claiming the physical presence of a flying saucer may simply be a step towards another, deeper understanding of the nature of reality.

These splits are symptomatic of ideas and social groups organized around what we have called (at the beginning of the previous section) a 'secret'. A secret is a social relation which divides those who know it from those who do not; at its simplest, it creates a distinction between 'insider' and 'outsider'. But as an organizing principle, the relation is repeated at each level, so that a so-called insider will not know certain deeper secrets; there will always be, potentially, an inner core or higher level to which the seeker might be admitted. If we turn the perspective around, the secret is always in danger of being betrayed, of being glimpsed or overheard by those who are insufficiently prepared or otherwise unworthy of being admitted to the powers conferred by the higher level of understanding. And this is how the secret spreads, through imperfect understandings being shared, willingly or not, so that the secret extends its field of operation by contagion. This is knowledge of a quite different kind to common sense understandings on the one hand and to scientific learning on the other; everybody understands common sense, and potentially everyone may share in scientific learning, through instruction. Yet even if, in theory, everybody was 'in' on a given secret, it would still have these social dynamics of spreading and dividing, dissemination and exclusion, and the secret would entail different content depending on the position of the actor. The secret evokes a logic of testing, initiation and education, of things that can be shared with some – the elect – and not with others, as well as the prospect of future knowledge yet unsuspected. It therefore supposes a world unlike the world of common sense or of the sciences, a world which cannot be laid out for the gaze and explored, potentially, as a whole; instead, it supposes many possible paths through an infinitely complex world, leading to mutually exclusive potential fates.

Considering the distinction between common sense and secrecy, it is possible to understand why intermediate-scale social energies are lost sight of and why Adamski presented the kind of apprenticeship he advocated as a dialectic between individual commitment and a universal account of the Cosmos. This observation returns us to the nature of the reductions performed by this style of thinking and to the work it performs. How should we characterize conspiracy theory as a pattern of thought? At a general level, it has two aspects: it eliminates any consideration of social phenomena and, indeed, of history (in imitation of a positivist scientific approach) and, in apparent denial of this elimination, it is constructed as a rhetoric of persuasion, seeking to recruit non-members to join a located group sharing what we may call a common lifeworld. Following discussion of the first aspect, the elimination of the social element, I will comment on the common sociological features that accompany that model and then, in the following section, after considering the rhetorical characteristics employed, we will examine the model of language that underwrites these features.

The elimination of the middle scale

The distinguishing feature of this kind of thought is best summed up as a contrast in scale between the broad scope of the imagination at work and the individual who enacts its vision, and the lack of any intermediate scale to mediate between these levels. It is an instance of the dilemma of having nowhere to go to seek explanation except either to the individual and their intentions or to the concerns of the Universe. Under these conditions, each principle discerned contains paradoxical elements. We have met these paradoxes in terms of beliefs and experiences. On the one hand, divisive energies are expressed through universal truths, so that proclaiming an ethic of brotherhood and service has the effect of creating its opposite, for it contains criticism of the existing social order and an invitation to reform and reorder it. Beliefs of a universal kind generate opposition, create separation and cause relationships to end. On the other hand, extraordinary events – singularities, incidents, sightings, meetings – rather than separating, serve to join people (and times) together, forging new linkages, associations and liaisons. Yet, while theosophical theory describes this re-ordering of connections at multiple scales, in practice, the new relationships are small-scale, fragmentary and insecure.

For, although the claims of the universalist theory are set out in terms of brotherhood and service, the energies associated with this social form appear principally to be expressed and lived out in identifying enemies near at hand. Again, we must distinguish between the scale at which the group's imagination operates and the scale at which it is realized (a distinction important to Harding's discussion of Protestant life forms – Harding 2000). Although the failure of projects and the recalcitrance of life to produce desired outcomes can be blamed on ill-defined general forces of opposition, in practice instances of betrayal of the secret by close associates readily stand in for these wider forces. Parties within the group or critics close by, who claim to share in the experiences but who differ in interpretation, can readily be taken to represent forces in the wider society. The activities of the press can lend amplitude to these imaginings. The possibility of paranoia and, as its accompaniment, conspiracy, come from this mismatch in scale between the actors as bearers of support or opposition and representations of their significance in the collective imagination.

The crucial formal feature of conspiracy theory is that it lacks any account of intermediary mediating structures between the interactions of individual intentions or wills and the broad scale, indeed, universal, narrative within which interpretation is offered. In Adamski, there are two stories in tension: on the one hand, the empirical level, the observations and physical details, the technology, the evidence – photographs, hieroglyphics – together with visits from security men and hints from military engineers, and on the other hand, the critique and hope offered by the teachings of the spacemen, the criticism of American culture and the dangers to peace, the participation in American metaphysical understanding (cf. Albanese 2007; Bender 2010). We simply move between the two, without reflection. Individual differences within the group can become interpreted as instances of vast influences in this fashion because nothing stands in this account between the individual will and the scale of the Universe, despite the multiple levels at which the Cosmic Mind is realized.

How might we further characterize the formal features of conspiracy theories, before looking at the rhetorical achievements of such a worldview? We can start from the ability of a conspiracy theory to absorb any new fact in its scheme: it can account for any circumstance by adding another factor to the explanatory narrative. As we have seen, Adamski's repeated failure to deliver convincing evidence was explained by introducing the notion of a split emerging among the spacemen and the feeding of misinformation to previously reliable witnesses. In a like fashion, Keyhoe explained every detail of his narrative by reference to a changing story of the divisions and policy changes among security men, a story which however remained concealed from sight.

There are three presuppositions needed to make this kind of thinking work (cf. Althusser 1969: 56–57). First, it reduces any system to its elements, assuming that an event may be understood by taking it in isolation and making a correlation with another isolated event, separated from it in time and space. The claim that Adamski started making unreliable predictions because of a change of policy decided amongst the spacemen is an example of such an eclectic approach. Lying behind this analytic presupposition, there is a second, teleological narrative, teleological because it leads to the revelation of the 'true' state of affairs; there is a secret story of origins and objectives which determines what count as elements and offers an evaluation of them. In our instance, the spacemen are seeking to educate humankind in their cosmic role. These two presuppositions – analytic and teleological – depend on a third, that the world we are considering contains the principle of its own intelligibility, that it is bounded and self-sufficient. In short, such a way of thought is marked by a superficial eclecticism, the sense of its elements is granted by a teleological theory, and both are guaranteed by its self-contained intelligibility. In the next chapter, I called this 'serial' thinking.

Although conspiracy theories may be extreme expressions of it, this form of thought is widespread: we often assume a self-consistent milieu of ideas and explain its productions by relating isolated elements according to narratives of origins and destinies. Ideas are supposed to bless or curse, to have benign or malign effects, and Adamski's account of strange events, various conspiracies and men-in-the-know is only a clumsy version of this approach.

It is more difficult to construct an alternative approach than it might seem at first sight, and this is because a second account not only has to give another, more persuasive, description of the facts at issue and their connections, but also must explain the force of the misreading offered by the paranoid account without recourse to its ad hominem themes. In short, we need to supplement serial or narrative thought not only with an account of structure or comparison, but also comprehend the dimension of transformation. We need a sociological account of the whole picture, including the investigator among the actors, rather than relating elements drawn from it: a reading rather than any simple description. The first step towards such an account is to ask what Adamski might mean when he made a series of claims and, more broadly, what allows the rival claims made in a milieu such as that of which Adamski formed a part. Meaning demands a setting against which it makes sense. Instead of making eclectic judgements based on resemblance, we need to pose a shared way of making sense in and of the world, an organization of elements. Then, rather than appeal to a teleology which arbitrarily gives sense to the elements selected from an outside perspective, we would explore that organization of intelligibility, identifying the elements actors chose to give value to and noting the various attempts they make to establish contacts and to persuade others of the outcomes desired. In short, the way of making sense is deployed in a setting made up of others to whom claims are made and from whom recognition is desired. And rather than imagining this focus on meaning, claim and recognition exists in an isolated and self-sufficient system in which belief and experience may be matched in a one-to-one correspondence, we are concerned with a concrete, actual history in which independent developments may create new possibilities to be exploited and where, because of the multiple options available, new things may emerge and human intelligence can have its play. I put matters in this fashion, rather than invoking conventional notions of structure, collective representations and social context or their equivalents, because we are not dealing in rules and predictions but, at best, with sharing in the practice of the subjects of our concern, making sense of human and non-human production, with discerning patterns in human behaviour retrospectively.

A parallel study

Courtney Bender offers a sophisticated instance of this approach in her study of New Age practitioners in Boston in the early 2000s, a study which brings out the complex social morphology to be found in a milieu with similarities to Adamski's (though more recent). Its value for us is four-fold. First, she brings out the centrality of the category of individual religious experience to this way of life; the groups are organized around the production, practice and articulation of encounters with the 'real', in 'Numinous unexpected experiences, mystical experiences of "flow", and daily synchronicities, dreams, and the like ...' (Bender 2010: 2).[25] Moreover, as she points out, this focus on experience has a long history, and is the principal characteristic of what has been termed American 'Metaphysical' religion.

Then, through ethnographic descriptions of apprenticeships and the collective construction of such notions as a second body, astral travel and reincarnation, she gives an account of how this focus on individual experience can be collectively produced yet is articulated without reference to the social milieu in which it is learned and the historical tradition it reproduces. The practices of contemplation and remembering, reviewing

25 These comments draw on Bender's Introduction, 'Long Shadows'.

patterns and discerning significant encounters, seeking new experiences and re-interpreting one's history in a continual renewal of the self, are all constructed around ignoring the middle-order practices shared by the teachers and fellow students who together replicate and re-enact these recognizable traditions. She notes more generally that through focussing on how experience works, practices of this kind 'simultaneously reproduce and hide their genealogies', and that there are more ways of participating in and transmitting traditions than using conscious memory.

Third, Bender demonstrates the ability of such groups to incorporate aspects of the surrounding society to assist and lend conviction to their thought, including developments in the sciences and social sciences, and the power these 'entanglements' have to create a world which draws in the anthropologist. In this approach, she explores the way words are used, a topic to which we will return, drawing on Favret Saada's insistence that there is no neutral position for the enquirer into matters of life-changing significance (Favret-Saada 1980): despite the seeming emphasis on the individual, there is a strong set of relations which interprets the outsider's show of interest, evaluates it and places her in relation to the concerns at issue – a series of social processes that are made invisible by assumptions about individual choices and pathways.

The last topic develops one aspect of the preceding one, for it suggests that the categories of outside enquiry – particularly those of sociologists, social historians and psychologists – take up the indigenous categories or, even, adopt them from the angle by which they present themselves. Intellectual thought is shaped by and reproduces aspects of these claims, notably taking at face value the notion that there is an ahistorical, asocial core of individual experience to any religion, presuming that religious social forms build upon indescribable exceptional encounters. In this fashion, both the histories told of these kinds of groups and the methods used to investigate them – interviews, surveys and the like – reproduce the groups' presuppositions without examination. This approach is then supplemented by attempts to correlate these attitudes with selected changes in the wider society, such as social 'fragmentation', the weakening of social ties, and so forth. This process precisely reproduces the situation we have described as missing the middle distance: much academic writing is occult thinking transcribed.

In brief, Bender has identified a series of themes that have emerged in this essay: the sites of emergence of social energies, their representation in terms of experience, which eliminates any reference to questions of social context and scale, the ability of such a narrative based on experience to incorporate features of the surrounding world, often conceived as oppositions, and the tendency of social scientific accounts to adopt aspects of the representations with which they are presented rather than to enquire into the processes of their production.[26]

If we map these concerns on the analysis of Adamski's life, we may notice, first, his concentration on experience, portrayed in encounters of various kinds, telepathic messages, and trips physical and astral. Then, the contrast between the social nature of formation, learning and new lives made possible, on the one hand, and the elimination of any acknowledgement of those apprenticeships and networks, on the other, by distributing all causes between cosmic stories (such as the instruction by Masters) and individual acts of will. Third, the bricolage of contemporary elements taken above all from military and technological sources and their deployment in a powerful system of discriminations capable of framing any passer-by or enquirer (the subject of the following section). And, last, the strong hint that many historical and sociological accounts of movements of this kind reproduce the central metaphysical presuppositions without reflection.

To summarize Bender's conclusion, we need to look to the institutions, languages and apprenticeships that produce the focus on religious experience, rather than exploring the categories that have been created, and this re-focussing leads nicely to considering the rhetorical force of utterances rather than their content.

---

26 The only caution I have with regard to Bender's approach is that she does not appear to ask whether these sites of emergence have specific social correlates; whether these social energies are hatched in one part of the social order rather than another, and how their improvisations spread and affect other, apparently more significant parts.

VII. A rhetorical account of language

As we have seen, Adamski simultaneously lives out and helps create a lifeworld which, while not a total account of the world, claims to identify certain crucial features which allow him both to orient himself and to act and to share this mapping with others. Although never fully consistent, this account appears to be both total and sufficient, and it is made more subtle by the fact that many of its more obvious claims turn out to be signs indicating less obvious truths (secrets). Part of its strength is that it recognizes only one world and one system of thought; it has no account of itself as a system of thought, nor any account of approaches which do not share its suppositions, other than error or conspiracy. In this fashion, it claims to be in every way a scientific account, experimental, open to testing, correction and revision. At the same time, it claims there is an underlying stable reality – the state of nature – which can be fully known. In short, it shares the suppositions of positivism, which permit the claims of a correspondence between experience and the organizing principles so that each confirms the other, the correspondence being revealed by the adoption of a method that explains the facts and confirms the theories within a perspective of continuous progress, as each part – data, concepts and method – adjusts to a more adequate mutual understanding (cf. Macintyre 1990: 20). Indeed, both approaches place a lot of weight in practice on the assumption of progress: the assurance that earlier understandings have been made obsolete. The difficulty with accepting Adamski's positivism lies, in a scientist's eyes, in the 'method' adopted to assure that advance, assumed to be the progressive revelation of the spirit of science, a synthesis of scientific method, which is both private and unverifiable, for election can only be 'verified' through embracing the position and exploring the imponderable claims at the heart of the position. It is possible to view this claim as a rival to the scientific vocation (see Jenkins 2013: 72–75); becoming a historian or physicist or geologist also involves a history of personal formation and an optic of disciplinary progress, but – in distinction to the occult account – the elements of it may be publicly shared. Much of the sense of conspiracy lies in the privacy of this claim of election, where meetings with spacemen occur not only because they have chosen their contact, conveyed instructions mentally and so forth, but also because they are enacting decisions made at the Interplanetary Council of Masters; a whole history of contact, initiation, interpretation and instruction is needed before the process could be understood. This distinction in kind between scientific and occult apprenticeship is probably best understood, however, in terms of location and scale, as to whether it is conducted within the orbit of big organizations – universities, industrial laboratories, military research establishments – or in their margins, and the extent to which shared ideas can be idiosyncratic or must, because of scale, be routinized.

An explanation of these practices of formation cannot remain at the two levels at which they self-present, summed up as the choice between acceptance or rejection of the empirical facts and the explanatory schemata. A great deal of work, however, has been expended at these levels, examining the plausibility of the facts and proposing other reasons for the experiences – misapprehensions of natural phenomena or psychological explanations (cf. Menzel). Instead, we need to look at the style of argument and how it generates its sense of conviction and horizon of hope, grasping the rhetoric of the worldview. We are not dealing in a total narrative, a self-sufficient explanation of the world and its effects, but rather a set of claims and a way of setting about things. The basic question is, what must be going on for these statements, claims and judgements to be possible?

In this perspective, the negative claims of conspiracy may be interpreted as symptoms of a rhetoric intended to persuade. This style of thought is met with initially through explaining failure, giving reasons why flying saucers have not been seen or photographs have failed to come out or explaining the non-appearance of spacemen at a rendezvous; we are offered technical explanations or pointed to policy shifts in the debates of hidden bodies or proposed tampering with memories and experiences by hidden agents. There are apologetic claims underlying these details: you should show willingness to be allowed to join in; you need to join in to gain insight; you must have been chosen to find these reasons plausible. Negative features are in fact pleas for a positive decision on the actor's part, so that acknowledging the plausibility of the facts is at the same time making a tentative commitment to the broad scheme of thought being put forward, allowing the possibility that things might be not as they appear but as they are claimed to be. Negative evidence, which outsiders may find unpersuasive, incomprehensible and even repellent, is part of a positive strategy, establishing the credentials of a reliable witness, developing sympathy between an insider and a possible recruit, and creating shared ground between speaker and hearer.[27]

A language of secrecy[28]

This question of the 'method' adopted by Adamski and thinkers like him can be explored with more precision in terms of a specific model of language and its workings. As we have seen, Adamski's group share many of what they take to be the assumptions of natural scientists: they take experience as primary and seek to test it, they look for independent confirmation of interpretations, and they are open to the revision of their ideas; in short, they subject themselves to the discipline needed to discover empirical truths. They also share features of the scientific approach to linguistic matters: they reject persuasion in favour of reference, and they subscribe to the formation of character by attention to truthful speech. The point of difference lies in their subscription to the imponderable nature of the secret around which the group is organized, symbolized by the notion of contact with spacemen, and this imponderable nature brings a second model of language – or language ideology – into play.

We have already met aspects of this model in terms of the work performed by the boundary between those who know (those who are 'in' on the secret) and those who do not and have noted how this distinction changes the nature both of instruction and participation. We have seen the implications of the imponderable nature of the secret for recruitment – how the secret spreads by contagion, by being shared with outsiders or overheard

---

27 In short, the three moments of ethos, pathos and logos – cf. Jenkins (2013: 3).
28 These paragraphs go over an argument presented in Jenkins (2013: 75–81).

or betrayed – and for group structure – which is organized by a principal of inward concentration, in a hierarchy of inner circles of ever more privileged knowledge. And under these conditions, language offers different possibilities than in the scientific model, and words play different roles.

We can identify three points of difference. First, language cannot reveal the truth in a plain way so that anyone might understand, and not everything can be put into words. Second, words mean different things according to the relative positions of the speaker and hearer with respect to the secret (this elsewhere is called 'perspectivism'). And third, hearing certain words may involve the hearer in unanticipated ways, for words, rather than conveying information, have power.

So, while scientific language is supposed to describe the world truthfully and objectively, to be accepted or rejected freely by the hearer according to his disposition or will, in this model of language words may have a power independent of the speaker and possess their own agency in the world: they may bless or curse. We have seen numerous instances of this in Adamski's accounts, in the ability of spirit communication by telepathy to summon, guide and instruct, in the direct effects of the Master's words on the hearers, restoring Adamski and preparing him (and, indirectly, us) for his tasks, in the hints contained around the function of proper names in the spacemen's world and in Orthon's brief utterance in 'one of the ancient languages spoken here on Earth', and in glimpses too of the malign effects on those who deny the messages (the Silence Group). In such a world, words depend on their context for their effects; they may be dangerous, or they may mean nothing, according to circumstance. An enquiry posed in terms of ordinary common-sense has to be tested; it will be met with an answer meant to deflect interest, but will also offer coded information, a symbol capable of being understood by the right person. Between people of knowledge, communication may bypass words altogether, taking the form of direct mind-to-mind contact, overcoming the constraints of materiality, space and time by telepathy. In the presence of a hostile speaker, a person in the know may be reduced to silence. In reality, most encounters lie between the extremes and are defined by the concerns of defending the secret, testing the intentions of enquirers and negotiating the possibility of recruitment. In imagination, however, there are rival powers at work – defectors, traitors, dark forces – and words can cause damage, always, however, to be discerned retrospectively rather than in the act.

Under these conditions, what emerges may be called a ritual language. It cannot readily be given a strong content, for it is organized around the emergence of a secret, one that relates to what we can call the collapse of problems of measurement into problems of definition. The language is produced under conditions of uncertainty, where previously secure forms of making sense have been undermined by technical innovations and sometimes in a situation of political conflict, and a different world of meaning, with alternative rules and experts, has been glimpsed in large part by re course to a religious and philosophical frame that was created at the birth of most of these modern forms of disturbance, by Theosophy, in the 1880s.

In this worldview, words are primarily concerned with marking boundaries and not with reference. Their purpose is other: they allow recognition and initiation, they place user and hearer within the orbit of a project and an organization focussed around that project, and they draw attention to the secret while keeping its meaning obscure to outsiders. Use of the language marks out the leader, who can manipulate this language, interpret new messages, and become an intermediary, persuading others and judging their reactions. The language marks out the follower too, who joins the community, receives the words, and explores their inner sense under the guidance of their instructors. 'Instruction' – which was Adamski's life's work – has more to do with integration into the group and recognition of leadership roles than it has to do with learning in a conventional sense, despite the erudition associated with this kind of movement, for the content is in practice poor. And the forms of language employed – the scientific vocabulary, the archaisms, the inversions, the occasional echoes of biblical style and motif, the expressions of awe, the attention paid to emotional states – all serve to mark the status of the secret.

In such a world, as Favret-Saada remarks, there is no possibility of neutrality: the actor takes up one position or another without meaning to do so; each person participates through action or inaction, words or silence. The notion of an objective, scientific description is simply one of the positions to be taken up, containing, as it does, an implicit evaluation of the various actors. Objective knowledge is no more than one of a range of tools to be deployed. This is a world in which personal knowledge, based in specific relationships, prevails over claims to universal significance (although it is presented in a series of universal claims). And in it, things, including words and silences, share agency with humans. As we have seen, words and silences are more to do with making and breaking connections than they are to do with reference, and so are bound up with estimating and evaluating the role and potential of both speaker and hearer. They depend on judgements made in each specific context and their subsequent review. In this perspective, words bind, forming new relationships and closing off others, and create new possibilities, which can be construed as desirable or undesirable, beneficent or harmful.[29]

The 'economy of words' employed by Adamski's group then expresses a recognizable account of personhood and social relations. If speech is active and words possess agency over and above purposeful human action, the person is not a bounded individual but a site where multiple influences and relations meet. The words and thoughts of spacemen, identical to spirits in this regard, are active in their hearers, causing thoughts, feelings and affects; they create new potential in their hearers, in effect, new persons. Words are parts of what has been called 'distributed personhood', a mobile state of affairs in which the self is made up of material acts and bodily effects of which he or she is only part-author. Moreover, these effects are not confined to the single actor; messages from spacemen work on a wider scale, establishing relations with wider bodies, altering collective destinies and, potentially, capable of sustaining life on Earth. Accepting the words you are given may alter not only the life possibilities of the follower but may also contribute to a better future for the planet and, indeed, the Universe.

29   It is worth remarking that once they have ceased to be active, words may be recorded in print and made public. Even here, however, they have an active potential in the possibility of persuasion and recruitment.

Final remarks

In these last two sections, I have offered a sociological analysis of Adamski's 'lifeworld', described in the earlier sections. The analysis focusses on the use of oppositional motifs to make claims and build a social order while at the same time denying any social construction, instead promoting an account of the human will, confronted by a Universe made in man's image, imagined as benign, self-conscious and creative. This cosmology is underwritten and supported by an animist theory of language. This self-accounting bears a family resemblance to the positivism of the history of ideas, which also seeks to join an analysis of individual intentions to notions of influence.

The play of family resemblances, though, can only be taken so far. In general terms, every worldview deploys ground rules which define a shared common human horizon, a sense of the community and its limits, and the possibility of individual action. Each worldview differs from other possible accounts in some respects while sharing other features in common, features which, because of the overall construction, will nevertheless hold different significance in each. The differences between worldviews, between say, a common sense position and an occult one, or between a positivist scientific account and a metaphysical perspective (of whatever hue), will be stark in certain respects and subtle and elusive in others. We cannot give a strong definition of any position that would allow an unambiguous ruling in advance of what is included and what excluded; theory cannot anticipate the empirical case. We can then only map overlaps, borrowings, incorporations, and oppositions between these fields in specific instances and in retrospect, and to do otherwise is to project the discriminations found in a specific setting more widely than they merit.

The classic distinction between reliable knowledge and opinion (episteme and doxa, 'science' and 'error') might best be made sense of in terms of what we may call social scale and density, the two variables of, on the one hand, the extent, size and complexity of the human setting and, on the other, the variety and number of human relations within that institutional setting. In small-scale settings, personal relations tend to predominate; in larger structures, broad conventions are needed; Durkheim said this a long time ago. In this perspective, more complex and worked-out worldviews will be the product of small-scale, dense human situations, whether we are talking of a laboratory within a big organization, or an occult group set in a more diffuse social stratum; both focus on novelty and its generation in a way other groups may miss.

Contactees – of which Adamski is the best known – bore a considerable burden. They were rejected not only by scientifically-minded deniers of any claim to the reality of UFO sightings, but also used as boundary markers by ufologists to decide whose claims should be taken seriously; in both cases, they were beyond the pale. Yet, by recourse to the imaginative powers of theosophical thought, contactees divined something of the conditions underwriting the certainties both of those claiming the reality of sightings and of those denying it. Under particular circumstances, when categories allowing measurement are suspended, fiction takes on certain supplementary powers, not only giving expression to this temporary condition but also exploiting resources which emerge in these moments, in this fashion contributing to the real. This conclusion at the small scale may be tested in the case of other, more recent, sightings.

CHAPTER 3

Machines and men

Given their initial involvement in the military-technical world, it is possible to see flying saucers as candidates in an experimental scientific process – as the interplanetary hypothesis, subsequently the extraterrestrial hypothesis – which took centre stage for a short while and were then discarded, but which continued to play a variety of roles (as discarded candidates tend to) in the recursive processes of scientific investigation. The possibility of there being interplanetary civilizations supports this approach. My concern now is to re-read the empirical narratives concerning the appearance of flying saucers outside the original context and to seek common themes.

We have examined two approaches from the early period to sightings of flying saucers, which at a particular point become termed UFOs. How might we refine these descriptions, and what do they have in common? The focus of this chapter is on the generative powers of these sightings, as distinct from the alternative forms of representation they offer. So, to pursue this reading, I will divide what is in practice a simultaneous 'event', embracing the emergence both of a new object and of its mode of registration (the report of a flying saucer), into two aspects: on the one hand, the generation of phenomena and, on the other, their representation: the emergent forms being grasped in different kinds of explanation. I focus on generation and largely leave aside any account of the problems of representation, although we also need some indications as to the broad themes concerning the processes of representation. The reason for making a separation between the aspects of emergence and covering over of an event is that each approach demands a distinct style of analysis. It is worth remarking there is also a further set of processes that could be taken into consideration, the becoming-routine of these representations and further shifts in their definition and content, but these too I will leave unconsidered.¹

I. Three forms at work in UFO reports

To summarize the story so far, we have considered two sites of 'writing something into existence', which we may call 'scriptoria'. And if we look at the context in which the case studies emerged, there are many other such instances, each evidence of a productive power. As a starting point, there were science fiction accounts of precisely this feature, describing the effects of technologies of recording and replaying and offering descriptions of a world constructed through the technical control of appearances, one where life was lived through a range of experiences and signs that were organized employing such varied means as architecture, drugs, images, advertising slogans, and popular media, and where there also was fragmentary evidence of monitoring the success of these manipulations and targeted interventions in the case of failure. Behind appearances, one might deduce, there was the benign or malign intent of the state apparatuses, although there were no clear indications of the interests at work in the images and so forth broadcast, nor in the apparently arbitrary and unreported interventions. The task of the awakening individual was then to get behind the appearances and go beyond what he or she was being told, to learn to decipher the political reality at work concealed by the signs produced by the technical apparatus. This description of the world was consonant with features of the everyday experience both of civilians and of returning servicemen in post-War America.

These features of everyday experience supported two related responses. On the one hand, a dualist worldview which could detect

---

1   The problems of representation are considered in the last essay, *Images of Elsewhere*, and the processes of development and routinization of the images are the business of the fifth essay, *Alien Sightings*.

conspiracies – hidden causes – behind appearances in a wide range of events. On the other hand, an understanding that the world possessed no secure meaning of itself, for it was reduced to a series of value-free facts, and the correlate sense that meaning could only be created by small-scale initiatives, either on the part of the feared conspiracies – government sellouts of various kinds, or communist plots, for instance – or on the part of groups which offered an understanding of the world and its organization, a world-secret, often constructed along the lines given by the theosophists, transmitting a certain counter-measure to the fragmentation created by scientific utilitarians and positivists. These responses may best be understood as theodicies which locate responsibility for meaning in restricted zones within society.

It is worth adding that flying saucers were not controversial in the sense of being technically implausible to any party: there was nothing remarkable about them. They were composed of an amalgam of elements drawn from contemporary technological and semiotic possibilities, made up of a mix of experience and speculation around German rockets, new types of aircraft, novel forms of propulsion, the properties of objects on film, and so forth. And they played too with notions of life from elsewhere which were commonplace in both educated and popular circles, notions of interplanetary beings with an interest in human activities, particularly in the context of global conflict and the production of atomic weapons, with a watching brief and undeclared intentions. Speculation included their being forms of life greatly in advance of our present technical civilization, regarding us benignly (a view deriving in large part from Blavatsky), with a minority view that they might see us as property, from the perspective of farmers or colonists (after Charles Fort; few people read H. P. Lovecraft in the period).

Once these objects began to make their appearances – and they did not have to wait for 1947 and Kenneth Arnold's sighting, with the appearance of 'foo fighters' by late 1944 and 'ghost rockets' over Sweden in 1946 – they became the concern of a second 'scriptorium', a systematic investigation created by Air Force intelligence. In that forum they were given substance through a series of technical fixes, centring around the deployment of home-based radar systems, and then transformed into a largely internal security issue, in a manner deeply consonant with science-fiction-influenced paranoia, being linked with potential threats to mass psychology and to be met by public education and action through the media, advertising and the like.

Certain episodes in the early history of flying saucer reports investigated by the Air Force played an important role. The striking feature of such incidents was the uncontrolled and unforeseen consequences for all parties of these encounters with flying saucers, in brief, the taking-on of new properties by both individuals and organizations. In the first place, the actors were caught up in a complex process including evaluation of their character, the establishing of common ground with a variety of audiences, and the plausibility (or otherwise) of the narratives proffered. This is in fact a general feature of social life: although the processes are never completed or fully agreed, each actor and institution puts forward claims as to worth, conviction and truthfulness, hoping to be taken at their own estimation, claims which are appraised and contested in different parts of the public arena. The consequences of an encounter with flying saucers, however, go further; in the second place, individual life trajectories became altered through these encounters, some actors receiving a calling, others a rebuff, opportunities of different kinds for a third group, inflections which would have an enduring effect within the person's career and activities. We have examined three such cases in the persons of Keyhoe, Menzel and Adamski. In short, different fates emerged. In this regard, individuals' lives recall the testimonies given to Orsi concerning encounters with the 'real presence' of the Madonna of 115th Street (Orsi 2010): a healing, a promise made and kept, an alteration in pattern of life, a small miracle such as a conception, the sense of an attentive presence in an individual life.

In the third place, this kind of alteration can also be perceived in the military institutions involved, in a wide variety of outcomes. This was the evidence that particularly provoked Keyhoe. These alterations included the creation and coordination of new technological devices, a range of initiatives to collect and handle data, the pursuit of various studies (on intentional movement, for example), and the attribution of budgets. There were such phenomena as policies agreed between branches of the services, rivalries triggered within and between security organizations, the intermittent attention attracted of higher political levels, changes in atmosphere within organizations and the occasional reversals of hierarchical order, coinciding with the accumulation of records, memos and so forth on the one hand and the ordered destruction of documents on the other. These led to attempts to engage public interest, and also to manipulate public perceptions by recasting the past and offering restrictive interpretations of the present, with recourse to notions of mass psychology together with the suspicion of individual or collective hallucinations and even subversive intentions. Further effects included the exposure of high officials to public criticism, the initiation of independent press investigations, and even the commissioning of a panel of scientists to produce a report. And, at the extreme edge, one can remark the monitoring of UFOs in terms of an emerging pattern of powers and behaviours ending up with quasi-magical properties of both mental and technological kinds.

After this business of 'writing into existence' in the early days and tracing the contrary process of 'writing out of existence', we find other scriptoria emerging in the same period, in the formation of flying saucer organizations on the one hand and, later, in the margins of the space industry on the other. In the latter case, there was a parallel history to the rise and suppression of flying saucers in the Air Force in the development and then dispersal of searching for signs of extra-terrestrial intelligence: the gradual adoption of budgets, the creation of means for the search, both the production of equipment and the construction of languages meant for exchanging information, and the development of what can be called a new 'epistemic thing', a complex technical image subsequently caught up in the development of new forms of thought. This history has also been mapped in the productions of part of the science fiction milieu. We met the dawning of the former, the interest of ufologists, in the earlier chapters.

All these kinds of new activities, capacities, projects, possibilities and potentials emerged with the assistance of encounters with flying saucers and encompass every level of society, from the ordinary citizen to the highest ranks of the armed services and of government. How might an anthropological approach help analyse this outburst of diverse productivity? What characteristics, broadly defined, are taken over from the military sphere to the civilian, and from the early history into later appearances?[2]

Two possible anthropological approaches

A longstanding anthropological topic has been the analysis of styles of relationship between humans and other creatures as a means of identifying different ways of being in the world. The notion of distinct forms of 'social logic' lies at the heart of the discipline, and it would be plausible to date the origin of modern social anthropology from the period of the publication of Lévy-Bruhl's *How Natives Think* in 1910 (proposed by Malinowski 1926). We are not concerned with that history, but the topic may usefully be extended to include how men relate to machines for, in this instance, like animals, spirits or angels, machines are thought to exhibit social dimensions.

In anthropological analysis of this kind, there are two broad styles of representation. They can be characterized in a variety of ways; we might call the one 'organic' and the other 'mechanical', although here I shall term them 'series' and 'structure'; the first which starts from the parts within a whole and focusses on similarities between elements and their transformation one into another, the second working at a more holistic and abstract level, comparing relationships within one series of elements with those found in another. Lévi-Strauss offered a summary of these discussions in *The Savage Mind* (Lévi-Strauss 1966: 223–228), identifying two distinctive ways of construing the world, the opposition of 'serial' to 'structural' thought. The series joins together heterogeneous elements and seeks the term which allows their relationship; it grades resemblances, finally arriving at an identification of man and his 'other' in mystic communion. The structure, on the other hand, breaks with the business of correlating appearances and instead proposes a second kind of social logic, emphasizing the differences

---

[2]   The following discussion is in large part an exposition and application of the arguments presented in Deleuze and Guattari (1980, chapter X).

between kinds and seeking instead to compare homologies internal to one kind with those internal to another. In the materials we have drawn on, sightings begin with resemblances and hints of the transfer of powers, with craft that might be of human manufacture, but which display extraordinary technical capacities and intimations of reading human intentions, anomalies which are subsequently controlled by being recorded, assembled and classified as a range of types, and compared with human arrangements, as (for example) small craft to mothership, likened to aircraft to carrier. These are serial relations, allowing the connection of man with a range of non-human variations, culminating in the controlling intentions of the Cosmic Mind.

Lévi-Strauss rejects the series in favour of the structural approach: it is not the case, he says, that 'men are crows' or 'men are red parrots' because both go on two legs (which is an instance of resemblance, allowing substitutions), but rather that the members of Clan A are to be distinguished from those of Clan B as crows are distinguished from swans, or as are parrots of two different species. To claim 'men are crows' is to mark a social opposition by recourse to a natural distinction. In this account, series are one thing and structures are another: men and women live their lives in the first mode, by and large, but the scientist understands the social and mental processes underlying the myths by which they live.

This distinction between two styles of representation or worldviews, 'mythic' or 'metaphysical' on the one hand and 'naturalistic' on the other, offers a powerful tool. It contains a view of time, that the primitive world view will be replaced by the modern, scientific account. Nonetheless, the distinction has its limits, for in practice these forms are found together: it is not the case that flying saucer enthusiasts hold one view and technicians, scientists, engineers and security experts hold the other in any exclusive fashion. The method of residues is an index of this mixing of styles of thought, employed both by the Air Force's UFO project (Project Blue Book) and by investigative journalists such as Keyhoe. This method examines each case on its merits, eliminates every instance that can be explained by natural causes, and identifies a core or residue of unexplained cases. Yet these unexplained cases can then be invoked in support of the interplanetary hypothesis, that the vehicles are intelligently controlled and that they come from another, technically advanced, civilization. These deductions can be further supplemented by speculation as to the intentions of these advanced beings, supposing them to be aware of recent human activity and to have noted the development of powered flight and the potential for space travel, as well as advances in the field of nuclear research and the power of nuclear weapons, and attributing to them the desire to reform and guide the human spirit through a programme of progressive self-revelation and education as the human race gains the capacity to interact with other worlds. And there is also fragmentary evidence of advanced mental powers to match the technical achievements of these observers. It is possible for any of the actors involved to stop at any point on this spectrum and to hold – with conviction – that the scientific evidence supports this position and no further.

In this fashion, although beginning from gathering evidence and controlled questioning of the material forms, resemblances in technological detail not only led to extensive patterns of similarity but also to interaction with wider purposes, leading to potential encounters first with more advanced 'peoples' and then, through them, with a Cosmic Mind. For as well as supernormal powers entering the picture, with the saucers' ability to read human minds and intentions, there was also the transmission of gifts, so that lives were changed and callings shared. This is a teleological form of thought, a variant on the long-existing theme of the Cosmos becoming aware of itself in the thought of the scientist, a form that is compatible with, although not identical to, the darker myths contained in science fiction stories.

It is also worth pointing out that scientific refusal of these extrapolations through resemblance, wherever the decision point is set, serves as nothing more than a refusal: it does not offer an explanation. The approach of 'seedings', employed by Menzel, by which natural causes may potentially account for every sighting, fails on two counts: on the one hand, it is always open to creating a residue of unexplained cases and, on the other, it offers no account of the generation of the frame of reference or reception of these seedings, having recourse only to gestures towards such vague concepts as mass hysteria, self-hypnosis, or hallucination. The choice for scientific scepticism is in this instance a rhetorical seeking to persuade the hearer to join one position rather than another along the spectrum.

Last, neither approach helps us focus on the generation of effects through encounters with flying saucers; neither series nor structure allows for the transitory nature of the altered conditions that accompany such appearances. Both forms of representation depend on stable second-order rules which permit speaker and listener to make sense, and these categories of apprehension are what are at issue in the event concerned. Neither form allows us to grasp the energy or life is found in whatever it is that are called 'flying saucers', their capacity to alter human lives, to bring new resources into play, to break off some relationships and to create others. We need to focus on the processes of emergence and shifts in classification that are logically, though not temporally, prior to representation, in this fashion getting 'behind' the work of language of interpreting, though at the same time not neglecting the power of language actively to contribute to 'making sense' in the world. We are then concerned with the processes of emergence and registration which together constitute the 'event'.

In sum, the common strategy when confronted with an anomalous incident is either to place the event in a comparative frame – 'this is a case of X' – or to include it in a narrative which reveals what is going on so that the audience appear to understand the 'true' significance of the event better than the actors or, at least, in advance of the latter's realization of their deception. The two options for representation, broadly speaking, are structure or series, comparison or narrative. In both cases, the bystander is supposed to understand the actors better than they know themselves. We are concerned to follow a different tack; although both modes of understanding play their role in the accounts leading to this discussion, my ambition is rather to give full value to the understanding and power of initiative of all those taking part, actors, audience, and investigators alike. We are at some distance, then, from any sorting of 'better' accounts from 'worse' or endorsing one kind over another. Neither narrative nor comparison has the last word; we are concerned rather with transformations.

'Generation': The aspect of the 'event' prior to representation

I have developed this focus on the transitory nature of events elsewhere in terms of the distinction between 'prediction', conceived as based on extrapolations from stable presuppositions (which permit representation), and 'prophecy', which might be termed a response to the collapse of certain such presuppositions and the glimpsing of new grounds of making sense (see Jenkins 2013, after Ardener 2007). In the present instance, I want to explore the contribution made by Gilles Deleuze,[3] who lays out the distinctions with which we are concerned between series and structure on the one hand and events on the other and offers three comments.

In the first place, Deleuze points out, as we have seen with respect to flying saucer reports, that the two forms of series and structure are complementary logics rather than the alternatives Lévi-Strauss claimed for the purposes of his argument and, further, that the distinction has a wide range of reference, for many both scientific and humanistic styles of thought can be arranged in such pairings as homology and analogy, descent and function, or origins and influences, which play on the pair of logical forms identified. The temporal argument of one form giving way to the other is unconvincing. Given the complementarity between the two, Deleuze suggests that the real contrast between mythical and scientific thought may lie rather in one being a creation of non-state social organizations and the other in the service of the state or allied with its interests. We should bear that last suggestion in mind.

In the second place, the profound reason for this complementarity is that, despite their differences, both series and structure are forms of representation. The one depends on a series of imitations or representations of the final (or the original) term, while the other depends on internal representations, imitations between the two series composing a structure, but in either case, comparisons are permitted because the World or Nature is considered as an immense mimesis, ordered by resemblance. Whatever their differences, and even antagonism, as forms of mimesis series and

---

3   I focus on Deleuze (rather than Deleuze and Guattari) for ease of reference.

structure are complementary and, indeed, have always existed together in various combinations.[4]

In the third place, then, from the perspective of our present interest – the generative nature of encounters with flying saucers – neither the series nor the structure will serve our purposes, for both are forms of representation and representation conjures away the character of the encounter as event, looking to questions of meaning rather than production or performance. The first option will not serve our purposes because the impact of flying saucers on the various actors and institutions cannot be well described or explained by the notion of a series of resemblances. There are of course a whole series of resemblances to point to: their machines resemble ours, as do their technologies (have they mastered nuclear powered flight, or do they possess anti-gravity devices?), and they are presumed to come from civilizations like our own except 'more advanced' in both ethics and sciences. But human engagement with them, seen in such effects as alteration of life course, gaining of mental powers, deflection of political interests and likewise of financial resources, alliances and fallings out of parties, initiation of technical projects and the like, can be seen neither as a fusion of kinds nor as a shared essence; there is no process of substitution. Although the engagement with flying saucers produces new phenomena in both human lives and institutions, these effects are not produced by the flying saucers being sacrificed for their human protégés, nor by their powers being absorbed into human projects, nor are they a staging post on the way to humans gaining new powers – although intelligence would like to understand the secrets of their advanced technology, and certainly there are stories of small corpses and captured machines hidden on secret airfields and the resulting development of new technologies.[5] But these forms of participation are never substantiated; the effects which are well documented occur elsewhere and in another fashion than by the mechanisms of the series.

4   Deleuze gives priority to the development of these forms of thought in natural history in the nineteenth century and suggests the understanding of social relations in the human sciences, whether in the study of dreams, myths or organizations, has been influenced by the scientific models (Deleuze and Guattari 1980: 288).
5   These stories begin with Skully (1950) (see Clark 1998: 206).

Nor can the second, structuralist option account for the kinds of human relations we find with these advanced technological objects. We might wonder whether structuralism's purpose is rather to deny their existence or devalue them, by breaking down these solidarities into two independent sets of relations, men on the one hand and machines on the other, with no necessary relation between. A structural analysis would define one series – past men, present men, future men, say – and compare it with another – past technologies, present technologies, future technologies – setting the comparison in an expanding world of knowledge and exploration. This juxtaposition would allow for myths of participation and substitution, a bricolage of present states projected into future possibilities and returned in novel forms, allowing longstanding hopes and fears about technology to be set against our enduring sense of ourselves as natural creatures (cf. Arthur 2009: 214–216). But the myths are to be *understood* in this account by a logic not of resemblance but of difference, seeking internal homologies and reversible relations. The structuralist introduces a formal correlation to allow us to distinguish 'men of today' from 'men of tomorrow' and to compare this distinction with that between 'technologies of today' and 'technologies of tomorrow'.

Classifications, as Lévi-Strauss points out, are codes allowing the comparison of existing objects and states; they have an objective legitimacy, and permit a revolution in thought, moving from the metamorphoses of the imagination (metonymy) to conceptual metaphors in the mind. The world becomes intelligible without recourse to any appeal, theological or other, outside the sphere of the human mind; the formalism of the structure replaces the teleology of the series. Yet, despite its power, this second account is also an impoverishment of the materials, not least in its elimination of any sense of time and change in favour of synchronous oppositions, which was the standard criticism made of the structuralist approach. It cannot do justice to the kind of productions outlined: the local effects associated with the reports of flying saucers.

Deleuze therefore identifies a third kind of social logic, prior to any form of representation, which we may call 'solidarity' or 'participation', and which we will now investigate. He offers a summary of the three forms under discussion: first, the series, to be found in rites such as substitutionary sacrifice and expressed in myths and stories; then, structures, exemplified in totemic institutions, which draw human and other worlds in parallel, and are expressed in scientific accounts; and last, solidarity, found in encounters and events and expressed in folktales and (we may add) science fiction, with their discontinuities and abrupt transitions (for the summary, see Deleuze and Guattari 1980: 291).

As a brief example of these three kinds, consider the well-known folktale of Cinderella. The story could be told either in terms of family concerns – transmission of rank and property between generations – or political rivalry – accession to high office. We have an account of the marriage of someone of high rank (a king), the birth of a child, the death of the first wife and re-marriage of the widower with a widow who brings her own children with her, and the subsequent concern about the interests of the child of the first marriage, with the resolution of Cinderella's problems and restoration of her status by an 'exceptional' marriage – in the face of competition from her step-sisters – in her turn. It is a story of enterprise and mastery of fate within the setting of a court and, more narrowly, a familiar family history. We could view the tale in terms of dynastic marriages and the passing of office and power between generations, with Cinderella at first gravely disadvantaged and threatened but then asserting her rights. We could also discuss the psychological and other aspects of the relationship between father and daughter, and how they resemble those between King Lear and Cordelia (cf. Collingwood 2008). In short, echoing Deleuze, we could construe the tale in terms of political, structural representations or in terms of oedipal, serial interpretations. But neither approach succeeds in portraying the mechanism of the transition nor the forces at work in the event. To attempt that, we have to take another angle and talk about the fairy godmother and the magical transformations she works to achieve her improbable ends, the alliances she enables Cinderella to make with various animal species, and the way these allow the young woman to make an anomalous connection, changing from scullery-maid into princess (although she is already a princess, despite appearances: she simply shed her disguise). There are clear limits to such an angle of approach; it is not a form of representation in that it lacks much content, but it recognizes connection, resourcing, and transformation. In this regard, folktales and the like are a way of mapping the social energies at work in an event, changes beneath the surface of orthodox representations, and deny the latter any authority of determination or priority.

I wish to analyse the materials gathered so far in a manner reminiscent of this last kind of literature, examining the powers and limits of the main actors to identify the processes at work and to set flying saucer sightings in a wider intellectual context.

A final remark: this approach appears to share a number of concerns with comparative mythology, exemplified in the field of UFO studies by Bullard (2000, 2010), whose original work was in folklore studies (see Bullard 1987). Bullard proposes what he calls a 'psychosocial' approach, arguing that 'UFOs ... owe most of their public character to a cultural version, to what human belief put into them rather than to what observation or scientific study reveals ... UFO ideas comprise a modern myth ... [that has] grown out of cultural traditions, psychological predispositions, and social preoccupations' (Bullard 2010: 12). He discusses specific cases by analysing the manufacture of narratives of UFO sightings through a series of stages of encounter, communication, and reception, bringing in the variety of actors involved, and pointing to the repeated recourse to a vocabulary of longstanding 'mythic patterns' (Bullard 2010: 51) which structure the resulting stories. He then gives a history of the evolution of a mythology of UFOs over sixty years, charting its 'growing stock of motifs, plots, characters, and themes' (Bullard 2010: 94), before tracing earlier appearances of such stock features in tales of medieval prodigies, signs and wonders, demons, Marian appearances, and a miscellany of Fortean wonders. He identifies the shift in location of such appearances 'from the otherworld to other worlds', which allows him to incorporate a range of anthropological, archaeological, classical, and folkloric fairy forms and abductions. And he analyses some specific, repeating mythical forms: the role of children in UFO sightings, the hopes and fears expressed in such reports more generally, and the very human accounts of alterity – of alien life – that they offer.

But there are some important differences with the approach I take here. For Bullard's work – a model of sober erudition – assumes a basic, universal human psychology, which maps new phenomena (about which, he makes clear, we know very little) in terms drawn from an inherited repertoire of myths which are to be found worldwide and far into the past. This approach defines every novelty in terms of continuity, seeking a pedigree to each new notion that appears. The structuring role of a science is taken on by comparative mythology and its mental associations of resemblance and contiguity, and any new thing, any appearance, is eliminated from the frame.

While resemblance is a valuable key, on which I draw, for instance, in the recurrence of theosophical ideas, it cannot be at the expense of historical particularity. Flying saucers, on the one hand, and abductions, on the other, have their own histories; they cannot profitably be projected back simply as instances of some wider condition. Although they have borrowed clothing from earlier events, they are also energetic productions, contributing to specific situations and contingencies as well as being produced by them, which deserve recognition in these terms.

In sum

The three writers considered, Keyhoe, Menzel and Adamski, share a good deal in common. In particular, they share a common worldview, constructed through technological innovation and in which suspicion of motives and paranoia are commonplace. But they place their bets on different models of language, each with a contrasting sense of its potential. While Keyhoe and Menzel mix serial and structural forms of argument, narratives and comparisons of relations, at the same time, they both subscribe to an understanding of language that supposes objective understanding to be possible in every sphere and science to be the sole arbiter of truth. Within this frame, they make contrasting claims, about the existence or non-existence of flying saucers. Adamski, on the other hand, explores the potential of another language model, one that acknowledges rather than denies the mutual involvement of actors and objects and thereby attributes powers of initiative to words, people, and things alike. He therefore puts more weight on narrative elements and less on questions of control and comparison, provoking a good deal of criticism and rejection.

As may be seen, we cannot simply map the social logics identified in the materials onto specific actors, although their examples bring out the contrasts between the positions. Keyhoe and Menzel, we might say, explore the resources of a realist position and struggle against its limits in different ways, while Adamski celebrates the power of the imagination to recast the possibilities of realism and go beyond its boundaries. He, curiously, is the most radical of the three. The lasting impression left by all three, however, is a sense of energy and the appearance of new things which demand engagement.

II. Solidarity and participation

What are the characteristics of this third kind of relation to machines? As a starting point, we may say there is a solidarity between the person who reports a sighting and the object sighted, between the machines allowing themselves to be seen and the response of the person making the sighting, a response which may include taking on qualities that were not previously theirs, for both the capacity to act and to understand are transformed. Rather than the neutral terms of 'observation' or 'encounter', we are better off speaking of an 'alliance' or 'participation'. In Kenneth Arnold's case, instigator of the first report, despite the public ridicule and a sense of persecution, he spent a lifetime following up other reports, making further sightings, and developing metaphysical insights. His story appears typical of sightings rather than exceptional (cf. Orsi 2010). However, to emphasize the argument of the previous section, this solidarity is neither structural, for it involves transformation, nor serial, for there is no confusion of essences. While the report-maker does not become identified with the other, the UFO or its pilots, nor does he remain identical to himself, for he takes on qualities which have nothing to do with an earlier self (though one can look for indications of predispositions, appropriate reading interests, membership of science fiction fan clubs and writing circles, or writing for pulp magazines, for example). He changes in what he knows, what he remembers and what he wants. He is involved in a process of alteration which Deleuze calls 'becoming' (*devenir*). 'Becoming' does not mean imitation or similitude; the report-maker does not become 'like' an interplanetary being. Nor does it imply a metaphorical process of comparison; it is not 'as if' the report-maker becomes such a being. Rather, 'becoming' describes a 'mode of individuation' that is brought about by the encounter with another form of life, a change in a person's fate.

Solidarity: from the report-maker's point of view:

If we continue from the perspective of the person making the report, certain features of the solidarity which concerns us may be brought out. In the first place, the report-maker is dealing not with an individual but with a multiplicity. Although there are many instances where a single UFO is reported, the sense is that we are dealing with an echelon, a flight, even a swarm, of machines, a collective entity. Neither the individuality nor the characteristics of the component members are of much importance and, indeed, UFOs are notable both for their variety of forms and for their plasticity: they can change from silver objects to lights and divide or fuse. Despite Keyhoe's attempted classification (1950b), it is not possible to define types of UFO as it is with aircraft recognition, nor to identify an individual machine as making a second appearance. Instead, as Hynek (1972) realized, they can be classified by the nature of the encounter the report-maker has with the UFOs or, as Deleuze has it, turning the perspective around, the 'mode of propagation' of the swarm, the way its effects spread through encounters.

For a person encounters flying saucers in the changes the machines call out of him or her, in the affects which are the expression of a multiplicity changing the self. This encounter is experienced initially in terms of a fascination exercised by the multiplicity, causing the report-maker to distinguish himself from the population of which he is a part, to 'individuate'. Arnold in in this regard a complete instance of an encounter and its effects, and it may be for this reason that the flying saucer moment precipitated around his sighting.

This single incident produced what in another jargon may be called a 'phase change' – a change in the ordering of a population of random events – and its effects spread by contagion: the impact produced by an encounter with one population precipitating effects in another. Notions of mass psychology were invoked precisely because of the contagious quality of the effects; we are not dealing in the orderly transmission of ideas, customs, orders and so forth through normal channels, but with the unintended conjugation of diverse elements and the production of short-lived hybrids. We saw above how the effects spread through a range of organizations, affecting the Air Force and the Press perhaps above all, but by no means confined to these. This is how we might begin to understand the role of images of encounters which both prompt changes in large organizations and cause these organizations to have to purge themselves of these effects. Changes of this kind travel across boundaries, bringing with them alterations in established classificatory systems – the collapse of previously secure orderings and the glimpsing of new orders.

The encounter with flying saucers therefore creates what Deleuze calls 'arrangements' within which a man pursues his fate.[6] A range of elements are brought together by the encounter: press men and their readers, intelligence officers from the military and other security interests, and a variety of technicians and scientists. At the same time, the report-maker, without necessarily intending to do so, becomes part of a society of those bound together by knowledge of a secret: they share insight into the flying saucers and experience of their calling (cf. Jenkins 2013). In Arnold's case,[7] he joined forces with the circle around Ray Palmer, linked up with Captain Smith, and spent time investigating other UFO sightings. He was no longer simply a businessman and a pilot, but shared different company and pursued different tasks. Festinger's account of the group around Mrs Keech awaiting the arrival of flying saucers in the Chicago area in 1954 offers insight into the life of such a society (Festinger et al. 1956). This new society is not bound by the rules of the state with its classifications, although the state finds ways

---

6 To determine comparable women's fates in the early materials would be a work of excavation; they are largely absent.
7 Discussed in the first essay, *Flying Saucers – An Introduction*.

of appropriating these new forms and putting them to work through its apparatus of bureaucratic means and technical developments, and nor is it an expression of domestic society, although the family too adopts flying saucers in toys and images. The group integrates machines differently to either of the other two styles; machines do not serve their interests so much as intervene actively in human lives, a style given crude expression in the covers of pulp magazines and their successors (cf. Kripal 2011). Crude expression, but no cruder than the pictures of high-tech machines in military or industrial journals of the period, nor in the images employed by contemporary magazine advertisements showing the family's domestic relations to machines. The technical journals are concerned with the classification of series and orders, and the domestic magazines with the narcissistic self-contemplation of the consumer family, while the third kind – pulps – deal in 'magical' machines, swarms, and effects. Together, they offer a fine illustration of the types of relation between men and machines.

A second perspective: from the UFO's point of view:

The perspective being developed focuses on interactions between groups, taking the individual primarily as the contact between populations, the point of contagious transmission which is experienced in new combinations and the opening up (and closing down) of possibilities. It is important to note that the model of contagion is not that of the spread of infective agents such as bacteria, but rather, as suggested above, a description of social mechanics in terms of systems theory and the idea of a phase change – although Deleuze's approach also comes from an engagement with Spinoza's project of considering 'human actions and appetites just as if it were an investigation into lines, planes, and bodies'.[8]

If the encounter is the point of contact between populations, we may ask, speculatively, what it looks like if we reverse the perspective and consider matters from the point of view of the flying saucers? The first thing

8   Spinoza's *Ethics* Part III, Preface.

to note is that, in practice, both terms in the relationship are changed, although we cannot know in detail the effects felt on the saucer side. At the least we can say that flying saucers show human-like concerns and interests, as well as many parallels with human appearances, technologies, and organizations. This double change is true of the mode of individuation or 'becoming' as a general principle; elsewhere, Deleuze calls the phenomenon 'double capture', where both terms in the relationship take on qualities (or affects) due to the connection while each maintains its independent identity. Examples of such 'social' processes abound in the natural kingdom, running from forms of symbiosis and 'mimicry' to competition, where adaptations are mutual and specific to the encounter between species populations, yet there is no question of confusion of essence. There is an asymmetrical taking-on of new properties on the part of each species, for each is caught up in a single process of becoming, a 'co-existence of durations' (Deleuze and Guattari 1980: 291) which does not have its parameters determined in advance.

These engagements between heterogeneous populations are not 'exchanges' but consist in mutual influence, and the engagement is dynamic rather than stable: it does not preclude involvements with further populations, although adopting one path may exclude exploring others for the duration, and both the nature of the effects – radical or otherwise – and their duration – enduring or brief – may vary. This mode of operation offers a model for the processes of mutual mapping and interpretation that constitute the social interaction making up 'everyday life' – the world of claim and evaluation. It can be applied, for example, to the mutual and intense relations between competing technologies and the role of intelligence in these engagements, which serves as a background to the writings considered in this essay. In this regard, flying saucer reports simply exhibit one of the features of broader social life, though one that is rarely focussed upon.

So far, we have concentrated on the relation between the report-maker, as a member of one population, and the swarm of machines, proposing that the relation is a product of the interaction between populations, expressed in affects, creating new capacities of understanding and action in each party. But in each report, the swarm of machines is encountered, and the contagion spread, through a single member or a small cohort of the multiplicity, which forms an alliance with the report-maker. From the latter's point of view, each alliance contains different possibilities and will be experienced in different ways, as pleasant or painful, and as increasing or, on the contrary, diminishing the report-maker's capabilities. From the collective perspective, the alliance is the point through which the effects of the multiplicity pass, the focus of contagion, where the influence of one population emerges in the affects of the other. Deleuze sees this process as the multiplicity 'deterritorializing'.

From the point of view of representation, or the reception of the process, the alliance is regarded as an anomaly and can be mapped in various fashions: in the domestic optic, it can be sentimentalized or condemned as an illicit union (as appears in accounts of abductions), or viewed in the optic of the law, it can be construed as a freak, breaking natural law, or as criminal, even seditious, activity in the context of the state. But these readings miss the work the alliance performs as a phenomenon at the boundary between populations, bearing affects which are seen in the alterations and disturbances that arise in both people and organizations, expressed in representations, reactions, and disputes.

The flying saucer that is the subject of the report is then best conceived not as an object interesting in itself but as the boundary which defines the multiplicity – the population of flying saucers – and that population principally considered as consisting in the interactions it engages in and the arrangements in which it takes part. Because the flying saucer observed is the defining point of growth and change, it can assume a variety of guises both with respect to the swarm (is it the leader, an exile or maverick, forerunner or scout of an invading horde, an emissary, missionary or teacher?) and to the report-maker (acting as guardian, guide or nemesis). And the horde led may be understood from the point of view of the arrangement put in place (envoys of an advanced civilization, scientists investigating human life, farmers or colonists sizing us up, refugees from a dying star …). This form of relation can then easily be misread by alternative approaches, and not only misread, but also undermined and taken over. The two dominant forms that reabsorb the boundary event are serial and structural representations, controlling the mobile point of contact by replacing affects with family feelings, sometimes mediated through medical and genetic concerns (this again points to abduction narratives), or with state or scientific concerns, looking to issues of intention and intelligibility. In a schematic fashion, the latter concerns appear in the early period of flying saucer reports (1940s–1960s), the former become prominent after that (1960s–2000s).[9] In Deleuze's terms, the deterritorialized affects which emerge from relations of solidarity between heterogeneous groups are continually threatened by being 'reterritorialized', recaptured by the representations of serial and structural modes of thought.

Leaving aside the topic of battles over representation,[10] there are two further points to raise concerning the alliances we have been considering. First, the report-maker steps away from domestic and official life by making the initial alliance, stepping outside human relationships to work out his fate with his non-human allies, but this is only a staging-post to forming new human relationships and activating human networks: animating varieties of flying saucer organizations, provoking debates between pro- and anti-saucer factions within military and intelligence organizations, generating press articles and mobilizing the opinions of scientists and other pundits, and engaging a wide readership. But we should remark that this stepping out and back is not a causal sequence performed in time but rather the two activities are simultaneous, for the second set of relationships – between saucer groups, the military-technical constellation, and the milieu of writers and their readers – guides the terms of the first, determining the capacities, conditions and gains in understanding which pass asymmetrically between the report-maker and the flying saucers. There is then a 'grammar' of what is possible and what is not: only a limited range of options can be called upon, and improvisations cannot be made at random, although equally they cannot be foreseen or predicted in detail.

In this fashion, flying saucer reports are a kind of small-scale politics, one that takes place outside the normal forms of organization of power, which are based either in such non-state organizations as the family or religion or else within state apparatuses. These interventions result in practical

---

9   One might compare Dean's periodization of space exploration in these terms (Dean 1998).
10 These are the business of the last two essays, *Alien Sightings* and *Images of Elsewhere*.

effects which are created within arrangements that are not familial, religious or of the state, but expressions of groups at the borders of these recognized institutions and hence anomalous, secret, ill-perceived movements that escape from the various orderings of society, therefore being forbidden and persecuted or else reincorporated, co-opted and domesticated. The alliances made with these machines permits anomalous activities between profoundly heterogeneous groups in society, illicit alliances, we might say, and the transmission of new capabilities outside the law (cf. Dean 1998).

The second point is yet more abstract. We began this chapter by concentrating on men's relations to machines because this was how the puzzle presented itself to us, but we have been led by the notion of solidarity to discuss the transformations of other relationships. What we might call 'machine-fates' are not so important; other fates come before them and still others succeed them; these alliances with machines arise from and lead to other sorts of engagements and affects. In a sense, all they do is allow certain things to be achieved, certain transitional positions to be gained. We might call these powers 'relays' to point to their transitional nature.

An alliance can never then be considered on its own, as a single, isolated event; each implies a string of such transformations, a continuous line by which the population or multiplicity changes. We have been looking at a specimen, a segment of such a line made up of the incidents and events that link together pulp fiction, sightings, Air Force intelligence, technicians, scientists and industrialists, the press, high levels of government, Security, and then parts of the space industry, not to mention members of the public. The interplay of organizations, milieus, groups and individuals is organized by this line of 'deterritorializations', which Deleuze also calls (appropriately enough) a 'line of flight': it forms a 'level of composition' in which heterogeneous elements becomes consolidated, co-existing with and succeeding one another in the serial and structural forms we can apprehend. The line, he suggests, is the imperceptible 'becoming-real' of the world.

With regard to the forms of representation, from one perspective they seem to be the origin and limit of the line of flight, for it escapes from the forms of representation and is continually recaptured by them; it appears to be both transitory and misunderstood. In another perspective, however, the line of flight is the possibility of the forms of representation, both the source of the life or force within representations and the basis of their ability to alter and change rather than simply to repeat. This is as near as we can get to speaking about the energy within the forms we grasp.

In sum

We have examined Keyhoe's adoption of a pragmatic, no-nonsense tone, Menzel's robust refutation of his claims, also in a realist style, and Adamski's extrapolation and subversion of these common-sense positions. Behind the exchanges of claims (reports) and denials, however, and the ongoing debate over which form of representation is appropriate to settle such matters, there is a process 'prior' to any description to be considered, which is then caught up in these debates and in endless disputes over interpretation. This process is acknowledged in part by the initial claim, despite its borrowing of positivist language, but resisted by the classification of kinds that attempts to strip the event of all significance. These materials are then appropriated by the imagination. These interactions, which take place at various distances from conscious apprehension, are to be found in the real world, and their marks are to be found in the literature. They are exemplified in the earliest debates over the appropriate means of understanding reports, and there condensed into the unresolvable alternatives of truth, error, or fiction.

Bibliography

Adamski, George, *Cosmic Philosophy*, Freeman, SD, Pine Hill Press, 1972 [1961].
Adamski, George, *Flying Saucers Farewell*, New York, Abelard-Schuman, 1961 [also published as *Behind the Flying Saucer Mystery*, New York, Paperback Library, 1967].
Adamski, George, 'I Photographed Space Ships', *Fate* 4, 5, July 1951: 64–74.
Adamski, George, *Inside the Space Ships*, New York, Abelard-Schuman, 1955 [also published as *Inside the Flying Saucers*, New York, Paperback Library, 1967].
Adamski, George, *Petals of Life*, Laguna Beach, CA, The Royal Order of Tibet, 1937.
Adamski, George, *Pioneers of Space: A Trip to the Moon, Mars and Venus*, Los Angeles, Leonard-Freefield Co., 1949.
Adamski, George, *Satan, Man of the Hour*, Laguna Beach, CA, The Royal Order of Tibet, 1937.
Adamski, George, *Saturn Trip I & II*, [privately printed], 1962.
Adamski, George, *Telepathy – The Cosmic or Universal Language*, [privately printed], 1958.
Adamski, George, *The Kingdom of Heaven on Earth*, Laguna Beach, CA, The Royal Order of Tibet, 1937.
Adamski, George, *The Science of Life Study Course*, [no place given], George Adamski Foundation, 1964.
Adamski, George, *Wisdom of the Masters of the Far East – Questions and Answers*, Laguna Beach, CA, The Royal Order of Tibet, 1936.
Albanese, Catherine, *A Republic of Mind & Spirit: A Cultural History of American Metaphysical Religion*, New Haven, Yale University Press, 2007.
Althusser, Louis, *For Marx*, Harmondsworth, Penguin Books 1969 [1965].
Ardener, Edwin, 'The Voice of Prophecy' [1989], in Edwin Ardener, *The Voice of Prophecy and Other Essays*, London and New York, Berghahn Books, 2007: 134–154.
Arthur, W. Brian, *The Nature of Technology: What It Is and How It Evolves*, New York, Free Press, 2009.
Ashcraft, Michael, *The Dawn of the New Cycle: Point Loma Theosophists and American Culture*, Knoxville, University of Tennessee Press, 2002.
Ashley, Mike and Robert Lowndes, *The Gernsback Days: A Study of the Evolution of Modern Science Fiction from 1911 to 1936*, Holicong, PA, Wildside Press, 2004.

Barker, Gray, *They Knew Too Much about Flying Saucers*, New York, University Books, 1956.
Bender, Courtney, *The New Metaphysicals: Spirituality and the American Religious Imagination*, Chicago, University of Chicago Press, 2010.
Bowart, Walter, *Operation Mind Control*, New York, Dell Publishing, 1978.
Branden, Charles S., *Spirits in Rebellion: The Rise and Development of New Thought*, Dallas, Southern Methodist University Press, 1987 [1963].
Bullard, Thomas E., *Abductions: The Measure of a Mystery*, 2 vols, Mount Ranier, MD, Fund for UFO Research, 1987.
Bullard, Thomas E., *The Myth and Mystery of UFOs*, Lawrence, KS, University Press of Kansas, 2010.
Bullard, Thomas E., 'UFOs: Lost in the Myths', in David Michael Jacobs (ed.), *UFOs and Abductions: Challenging the Borders of Knowledge*, Lawrence, KS, University Press of Kansas, 2000: 141–191.
Cantril, Hadley, *The Invasion from Mars: A Study in the Psychology of Panic*, New Brunswick, Transaction Publishers, 2008 [1940].
Chiang, Ted, 'Story of Your Life', in Ted Chiang, *Stories of Your Life and Others*, New York, Vintage Books, 2002: 91–146.
Clark, Jerome, *The UFO Book: Encyclopedia of the Extraterrestrial*, Detroit, Visible Ink Press, 1998.
Collingwood, R. G., *The Philosophy of Enchantment*, Oxford, Oxford University Press, 2008.
Dean, Jodi, *Aliens in America: Conspiracy Cultures from Outerspace to Cyberspace*, Ithaca, NY, Cornell University Press, 1998.
Deleuze, Gilles and Félix Guattari, *Mille plateaux*, Paris, Editions de Minuit, 1980.
Descombes, Vincent, *Proust: Philosophy of the Novel*, Stanford, Stanford University Press, 1992 [1987].
Descombes, Vincent, *The Mind's Provisions: A Critique of Cognitivism*, Princeton, Princeton University Press, 2001 [1995].
Favret-Saada, Jeanne, *Deadly Words: Witchcraft in the Bocage*, Cambridge, Cambridge University Press, 1980 [1977].
Festinger, Leon, Henry W. Riecken and Stanley Schlachter, *When Prophecy Fails*, London, Pinter & Martin 2008 [1956].
Fort, Charles, *The Complete Books of Charles Fort [The Book of the Damned, New Lands, Lo! and Wild Talents]*, New York, Dover, 2003.
Hallet, Marc, *A Critical Appraisal of George Adamski: The Man Who Spoke to the Space Brothers*, Published on the Internet, 2015, ia601305.us.archive.org.
Harding, Susan, *The Book of Jerry Falwell: Fundamentalist Language and Politics*, Princeton, Princeton University Press, 2000.

Hynek, J. Allen, *The UFO Experience: A Scientific Enquiry*, New York, Ballantine Books, 1972.

Jacobs, David Michael, *The UFO Controversy in America*, Bloomington, Indiana University Press, 1975.

Jenkins, Timothy, *Of Flying Saucers and Social Scientists: A Re-reading of When Prophecy Fails and of Cognitive Dissonance*, New York, Palgrave Macmillan, 2013.

Jenkins, Timothy, 'Secrets of the Spirit World', in Timothy Jenkins, *Religion in English Everyday Life*, Oxford and New York, Berghahn, 1999: 221–237.

Johnson, Maud Lalita, *The Sacred Symbol*, Laguna Beach, CA, The Royal Order of Tibet, [n.d.].

Johnson, Maud Lalita, *Transmitted Light – Latoo the Instrument, Lalita the Recorder*, Laguna Beach, CA, The Royal Order of Tibet, 1937.

Jung, C. G., *Flying Saucers: A Modern Myth of Things Seen in the Skies*, New York, MJF Books, 1978 [1958].

Keel, John, *Operation Trojan Horse: The Classic Breakthrough Study of UFOs*, San Antonio, Anomalist Books, 2013 [1970].

Keel, John, *Searching for the String: Selected Writings of John A. Keel*, Andy Colvin (ed.), Seattle, Metadisc Productions & Point Pleasant, WV, New Saucerian Books, 2014.

Keyhoe, Donald, *Aliens from Space: The Real Story of Unidentified Flying Objects*, New York, Doubleday, 1973.

Keyhoe, Donald, 'Flying Saucers Are Real', *True* 11–13, January 1950a: 83–87.

Keyhoe, Donald, *The Flying Saucers Are Real*, New York, Fawcett Publications, 1950b.

Keyhoe, Donald, *Flying Saucers from Outer Space*, New York, Henry Holt and Co., 1953.

Keyhoe, Donald, *Flying Saucers: Top Secret*, New York, G. P. Putnam's Sons, 1960.

Keyhoe, Donald, *The Flying Saucer Conspiracy*, New York, Henry Holt and Co., 1955.

Keyhoe, Donald, *The Vanished Legion*, New York, Age of Aces Books, 2011.

Kripal, Jeffrey, *Mutants and Mystics: Science Fiction, Superhero Comics, and the Paranormal*, Chicago, the University of Chicago Press, 2011.

Latour, Bruno, *We Have Never Been Modern*, Cambridge, MA, Harvard University Press, 1993.

Lepselter, Susan, *The Resonance of Things Unseen: Poetics, Power, Captivity, and UFOs in the American Uncanny*, Ann Arbor, University of Michigan Press, 2016.

Leslie, Desmond and George Adamski, *Flying Saucers Have Landed*, London, Werner Laurie and New York, The British Book Centre, 1953.

Lévi-Strauss, Claude, *The Savage Mind*, London, Weidenfeld and Nicholson, 1966 [1962].

Lévy-Bruhl, Lucien, *How Natives Think*, London, George Allen & Unwin, 1926 [1910].
Lewis, James R. (ed.), *The Gods Have Landed: New Religions from Other Worlds*, Albany, NY, State University of New York (SUNY) Press, 1995.
Macintyre, Alastair, *Three Rival Versions of Moral Enquiry: Encyclopaedia, Genealogy, and Tradition*, London, Duckworth, 1990.
Malinowski, Bronislaw, 'Anthropology', in *Encyclopaedia Britannica* (13th edn), 1926.
Melton, J. Gordon, 'The Contactees: A Survey', in James R. Lewis (ed.), *The Gods Have Landed*, Albany, SUNY Press, 1995: 1–13.
Menzel, Donald, *Flying Saucers*, Cambridge, MA, Harvard University Press, 1953.
Menzel, Donald, 'UFO: Fact or Fiction?', Prepared Statement for Symposium on Unidentified Flying Objects, Hearing before the Committee on Science and Astronautics, US House of Representatives, Ninetieth Congress, second session, 29 July 1968, to be found at <https://files.ncas.org/ufosymposium/menzel.html> (accessed 21 August 2020).
Menzel, Donald and Ernest Taves, *The UFO Enigma: The Definitive Explanation of the UFO Phenomenon*, New York, Doubleday and Co., 1977.
Menzel, Donald and Lyle Boyd, *The World of Flying Saucers: A Scientific Examination of a Major Myth of the Space Age*, New York, Doubleday and Co., 1963.
Moore, R. Laurence, *In Search of White Crows: Spiritualism, Parapsychology, and American Culture*, New York, Oxford University Press, 1977.
Moseley, James, in 'Special Adamski Exposé Issue', *Saucer News*, October 1957.
Moseley, James and Karl Pflock, *Shockingly Close to the Truth*, Amherst, NY, Prometheus Books, 2002.
Orsi, Robert, *The Madonna of 115th Street: Faith and Community in Italian Harlem, 1880–1950*, New Haven, Yale University Press, 2010 [1985].
Owen, Alex, *The Place of Enchantment: British Occultism and the Culture of the Modern*, Chicago, University of Chicago Press, 2004.
Partridge, Christopher (ed.), *UFO Religions*, London, Routledge, 2003.
Peebles, Curtis, *Watch the Skies! A Chronicle of the Flying Saucer Myth*, Washington, Smithsonian Institution Press, 1994.
Pendle, George, *Strange Angel: The Otherworldly Life of Rocket Scientist John Whiteside Parsons*, London, Phoenix, 2006 [2005].
Roth, Christopher, 'Ufology as Anthropology: Race, Extraterrestrials, and the Occult', in Debbora Battaglia (ed.), *E.T. Culture: Anthropology in Outerspaces*, Durham, Duke University Press, 2005: 38–93.
Rothstein, Mikael, 'Mahatmas in Space: The UFOlogical Turn and Mythological Materiality of Post-World War II Theosophy', in Olav Hammer and Mikael

Rothstein (eds), *Handbook of the Theosophical Current*, Leiden, Brill, 2013: 217–236.

Ruppelt, Edward J., *The Report on Unidentified Flying Objects: The Original 1956 Edition*, New York, Cosimo Classics, 2011 [originally Doubleday and Co., 1956].

Sardella, Ferdinando, *Modern Hindu Personalism: The History, Life, and Thought of Bhaktisiddhanta Sarasvati*, New York, Oxford University Press, 2013.

Satter, Beryl, *Each Mind a Kingdom: American Women, Sexual Purity, and the New Thought Movement, 1875–1920*, Berkeley, University of California Press, 1999.

Scully, Frank, *Behind the Flying Saucers*, New York, Henry Holt and Co., 1950.

Swords, Michael and Robert Powell (eds), *UFOs and Government: A Historical Inquiry*, San Antonio, Anomalist Books, 2012.

The Day the Earth Stood Still (film), 1951.

Urban, Hugh, *The Church of Scientology: A History of a New Religion*, Princeton, Princeton University Press, 2011.

Vallee, Jacques, *Passport to Magonia: From Folklore to Flying Saucers*, Brisbane, Daily Grail Publishing, 2014 [1969].

Weekley, Maurice and George Adamski, 'Flying Saucers as Astronomers See Them', *Fate* 4, 5, September 1950: 56–59.

Zinsstag, Lou and Timothy Good, *George Adamski: The Untold Story*, Beckenham, Ceti Publications, 1983.

Index

abductions 40, 116–117, 123–124
Adamski, George 43–101, 117–118
Adept 63, 65, 68, 77, 81 *see also* Master
Air Force, United States 5, 10, 12–14, 16, 28, 34–36, 36–40, 50, 52, 58, 79, 105, 107, 120
Althusser, Louis 89
APRO (Aerial Phenomena Research Organization) 39–40
Arnold, Kenneth 10, 15, 58, 60, 118–120
ATIC (Air Technical Intelligence Center) 28, 34–35, 39
autodidact 46, 82

Bender, Courtney 89, 91–93
biblical imagery 98
Blavatsky, Helena Petrovna 66, 77, 81–82, 105
blessings and curses 90, 97
boundary phenomena 123
broadcast of *War of the Worlds* 12, 22, 24
Brotherhood, Universal 54, 68–69, 71, 73, 84, 88
Bullard, Thomas E. 116–117

Cinderella 115
CISCOP (Committee for the Scientific Investigation of Claims for the Paranormal) 40
classification of UFOs 35, 62, 119
Congressional hearings 29, 39
conspiracy, conspiracy theory 8, 27, 32, 37, 39, 49, 79, 85, 87–90, 94–95
contact narrative 60–65

contactee 39, 44–45, 81, 101
contagion 2, 76, 86, 96, 120–122
Cosmic Mind 82, 89, 109–110
creation, unity of 71, 73

Deleuze, Gilles 106, 112–116, 119–126
divisions, internal 76
dynamics of small groups 45, 84–93, 101–102

error, explanation of 14–32, 94, 100

Favret-Saada, Jeanne 92, 98
FBI (Federal Bureau of Investigation) 9, 54, 58, 83
Festinger, Leon 81, 120
fiction 7–9, 15, 23, 32, 40, 101, 126
Film Noir 32, 38
flying saucer organizations 38, 107, 124 *see also* APRO; NICAP; MUFON
folk tales 115–117
Fort, Charles 21, 105

generation 110–117
Good, Timothy 75–81

Hallet, Marc 53–60, 77–81
Holmes, Sherlock 18–20
Hubbard, L. Ron 83

Interplanetary Council 77, 81, 95
interplanetary hypothesis 5–40, 44–45, 84, 103, 109

Jenkins, Timothy 29, 60, 76, 94, 96, 112, 120
John, Clara 38, 66
Johnson, Maud Lalita 54–56
Jung, Carl 32, 76

Keel, John 58, 76, 78, 80
Keyhoe, Donald 5–13, 32–41, 44, 62

language models 29–32, 94–99, 117
language of science 29–32
language of secrecy 96–99
Layne, Meade 57–58
Leslie, Desmond 44, 66
Lévi-Strauss, Claude 108–109, 112, 114
Lévy-Bruhl, Lucien 108
Loving Service 54–55, 68–69, 73

Master, Space Master 57, 59, 63, 65, 67–74 *see also* Adept
Menzel, Donald 14–32, 35–36, 40–41, 117–118
metaphysical religion 89, 91, 93, 100, 109
MUFON (Mutual UFO Network) 40

narrative and comparison 3–4, 90, 111, 117 *see also* series and structure
New Thought 57
NICAP (National Investigations Committee on Aerial Phenomena) 6, 35–40, 66

Orsi, Robert 106, 118
Orthon 71, 78, 97
OTO (Ordo Templis Orientis) 82–83

Palmer, Ray 50, 56, 120
paranoid style 2
Parsons, Jack 82–83
Philip Strange 7–9

Point Loma (theosophical settlement) 54
popular science in pulp magazines 15
primitive beliefs 18, 20, 27, 29, 109
pseudoscience 17, 22, 24, 27, 29, 45
pulp magazines 1–2, 6–7, 15, 63, 82, 118, 121, 125

radar 10, 14, 26, 34, 105
religious experience 17–18, 22, 91, 93
representation 3, 29, 93, 103, 108–113, 115, 123–126
Robertson panel report 23, 33, 36–37, 79
Royal Order of Tibet 54–56, 80
Ruppelt, Edward 10, 28, 33

Saturn Trip 77, 79, 81–82
scale 43, 73, 85–91, 93, 95, 100–101, 105, 124
science fiction 1, 15, 17–18, 24, 26, 45, 56, 58, 63, 76, 82, 85, 104, 107, 110, 115, 118
secrecy, sociology of 2, 60, 67, 76–81, 84–87, 94
series and structure 3–4, 108–114 *see also* narrative and comparison
Silence Group 37, 79, 85, 97
Skully, Frank 24, 65, 115
social logic, three kinds 3–4, 108, 114
spirit communications 56–60, 97
spirit guides 60
styles of thought: State, Familial, Generative 103, 109, 112–113, 115, 120–126
superstition 15, 18, 22–23, 25, 27, 55
Supreme Being 68–69, 73

telepathy 7, 64, 70, 72, 77–78, 97
The Day the Earth Stood Still (film) 44, 63
theodicy 2, 32, 46, 81

Theosophy, theosophical influence 2, 14, 45, 48, 52, 56, 63–66, 68, 74–75, 82, 84, 101
transfer (from military to civilian sphere) 1, 4
truth claims 6, 41

'unified state of consciousness' 59, 70

vocation, scientific 31, 94

Washington incident 23, 26, 33, 35, 80
Williamson, George H. 53, 57–59, 61, 66
writing into existence 104, 107

Zinsstag, Lou 53, 75–81

Mini Series: Images of Elsewhere
TIMOTHY JENKINS

Vol. I
Flying Saucers: An Introduction

Vol. II
Religion and Science Fiction

Vol. III
Martian Linguistics

Vol. IV
UFO Reports

Vol. V
Alien Sightings

Vol. VI
Images of Elsewhere

www.ingramcontent.com/pod-product-compliance
Ingram Content Group UK Ltd.
Pitfield, Milton Keynes, MK11 3LW, UK
UKHW021323180426
11947UKWH00017B/1406